Nop's Hope

BOOKS BY DONALD MCCAIG

Novels

The Butte Polka
Nop's Trials

Entertainments

Stalking Blind
The Man Who Made the Devil Glad
The Bamboo Cannon

Nonfiction

Eminent Dogs, Dangerous Men
An American Homeplace

Poetry

Last Poems

NOP'S HOPE

DONALD McCAIG

Crown Publishers, Inc.
New York

Published by Crown Publishers, Inc., 201 East 50th Street, New York, New York 10022. Member of the Crown Publishing Group.

Random House, Inc. New York, Toronto, London, Sydney, Auckland
CROWN is a trademark of Crown Publishers, Inc.

Manufactured in the United States of America

Design by M. Kristen Bearse

Library of Congress Cataloging-in-Publication Data
McCaig, Donald.
Nop's Hope / by Donald McCaig.—1st ed.
1. Parent and child—United States—Fiction.   2. Country life—United States—Fiction.   3. Widows—United States—Fiction.
4. Dogs—United States—Fiction.   5. Border collies—Fiction.
I. Title.
PS3563.A2555N55   1994
813'.54—dc20   93-41983
                                                                          CIP

ISBN 0-517-58488-3

10   9   8   7   6   5   4   3   2   1

First Edition

For Mr. Pip—
See you on down the road.

ACKNOWLEDGMENTS

I am indebted to the Border Collie community for their warmth and generosity. Thanks to those people who welcomed me into their homes or RV's, to those who found a cup of coffee on a cold morning, and to those who so freely shared their knowledge of dogs. Special thanks to those handlers who let me use their names and their dog's names in this book.

Real books are derived from the stories of real lives, human and dog. Thanks for entrusting me with your stories.

Nop's Hope

January 15, Fort Worth, Texas
Judge: Dr. Leroy Boyd, Starkville, Mississippi

22 Open dogs went to the post

1. Bud Boudreau	Patches	92
2. Herbert Holmes	Dave	91
3. Penny Burkeholder	Hope	85
4. E. B. Raley	Kim	84
5. Orin Barnes	Sioux	82

THE DOG WAS BETTER built for misery than the woman was. When the icy rain smacked his back, it clung briefly to the guard hairs before sliding off, and his downy undercoat kept him snug. In this low light, he could see better than she could and didn't misstep or stumble so often. When finally a pickup did come hurtling down the blacktop and she leaned out, pleading with her thumb, the dog narrowed his eyes against the headlights, and as it sluiced by, the empty stock trailer clattering behind, the dog simply turned his head. Clutching her ruined nylon jacket together, hanging over the asphalt, the woman caught the worst of the trailer's chilled rooster tail.

"Shoot," she said.

Three hundred yards down the road, the taillights were sucked up in the mist like they never had been.

Two trucks in two hours. The dog pushed his nose into the soft place behind the woman's knee, smelled her recent history: soured metallic sweat, adrenaline lees (which smelled like an electrical fire), and the faint hint of how her skin had smelled yesterday morning when she'd last showered. The dog smelled the cloak of her exhaustion. He made a noise in the back of his throat.

"Hush, Hope. It won't be so long until daylight."

In the daylight, the ranch land between Del Rio, Texas, and Meridian rolls softly in regular waves like a new furrowed cotton field. There aren't any houses beside Texas Farm Road 174, though every few miles ranch gates introduce the great acreages behind them. In a kinder time, before Dallas real estate speculators started gambling with hill country properties, these ranches were inhabited, each with its own dependencies, bunkhouse and big house, but during the last oil boom, the ranches were put into play. In good times these ranches turned over quick as they could be vacated and a new wooden brand hung over the gate. When the boom collapsed, the Dallas boys were stuck with land they'd bought for $750 an acre and couldn't sell for $500. Some bailed out, took what they could, depressed the prices further. Those who could, hunkered down, took their licking, and leased their land to working stockmen for whatever they could get for it—often no more than five dollars per acre, per year.

From Texas 174 on a clear starry night, you can see a few sodium lights out there somewhere, guarding empty workshops and ranch houses. On a rainy night in January, you can

2

only see the dark pavement, the sandy shoulder, the dead coyote smashed into the ditch, his broken jaws, the water backed up behind his matted gray body.

The dog was fastidious, shook his paws clear of the muddy water. His hackles settled.

"Come away from that, Hope," the woman said, wearily. "He's nobody's problem now."

Up the road a piece, Sheriff's Deputy Dwight Blanchard (age twenty-four) was thinking that life could be pretty funny sometimes. When his car passed Del Rio's "fly-in" bank, the deputy noted this injustice: that some fellows get to traipse around the country in Lear jets while other fellows go off to jail.

The windshield wipers worked at the rain, which would drizzle for five or ten minutes before pouring down. He'd use his defrosters to clear his windows and then it'd get too hot in the car, so he'd turn them off again. When WYGO "The Voice of Bosque County" played George Strait singing about country honeymoons, the deputy turned the radio off.

If there'd been anybody else to take Billy Lee to Dallas, Dwight surely wouldn't have gone but most everybody, from Sheriff on down, was the Stock Show.

He worked at the lid of his coffee cup until he had a slot open so he wouldn't dribble on his shirt, which he was hoping to wear tomorrow, having put it on fresh this evening at ten o'clock when it got to be inevitable who'd take Billy Lee to Dallas. Him and Billy Lee had been a year apart in high school and both played for the Bosque County Bandits. Dwight had been a guard on account of how he couldn't pass or catch very well. Billy Lee had played end. He always had been small and quick.

Dwight wondered how come if Billy was so quick he got caught all the time. Some of the other bad guys in Bosque County went on stealing for years and years and never did get caught, but seemed like Billy Lee, every time he came out of a convenience store waving a bag full of cash receipts there'd be a police car just pulled up for a six of Lone Star before going off duty. Billy Lee took it right, give him credit, always dropped his pistol like it was hot and grabbed for the air, never tried to shoot it out or run or anything. And now he was a habitual offender and his old teammate had put his papers in a brown plastic folder and cuffed Billy Lee and drove him to Dallas because his court day was Monday and he likely would be sent away to Huntsville Penetentiary. Thinking how his and Billy Lee's lives had diverged, reflecting on the lucky choices he had made—Dwight was past the old pickup before he properly saw it. He drove a half mile farther before he turned around.

Hood up, flashers blinking weakly, Virginia plates, camper top, nobody up front, rounded bubbly fenders, Dodge, '67 or '68? No bright orange sticker on the door, the highway patrol hadn't found it yet. The rain gusted up and Dwight waited in his car until the computer checked it out.

Wrapped in his yellow rain slicker he aimed his light into the camper part. Sleeping bag rolled up, inflatable mat, a Coleman stove, couple suitcases, half gone loaf of bread. Nothing up front but a blanket folded neatly on the passenger side and some kind of curved stick, like a stockman's cane in the rifle rack. The engine compartment smelled like burnt oil and Dwight wrinkled his nose. He attached the abandoned vehicle sticker and peeled off his slicker before he got in the car. He'd been on duty since eight o'clock last night, and when he got home he was going to have breakfast with Sally Anne before she went off to work at the school board. "Ships that pass in the night," was how Sally put it.

When he turned the radio on again, it was a commercial for Johnson's Farm Supply. "If you've got those frozen water pipe blues," the announcer said, "we've got the torches and heat tapes to cure them."

WYGO swung into a bluegrass fiddle tune, upbeat and sorrowful, and Dwight drove right by the Mexican and the dog, thinking that it was odd to see a Mexican walking a dog, wondering if it was something special about Mexican culture that they didn't take their dogs with them like white people did. Plenty of dogs around their houses, usually the skinny kind, but, to be fair (Dwight thought), he supposed some of the rich Mexicans in Dallas had dogs just as fancy as any white person did.

"God damn it to hell," Dwight said, and backed and sawed before he got himself turned around heading back the way he came. The way the Mexican had his thumb out, like it was *real* important Dwight stopped—that's what got him.

Because he was a cop and it wasn't entirely unknown for a hitchhiker to pull a gun out of his pocket and dispatch the helpful cop, he stopped well short of the Mexican and kept his high beams on him. Her? Awful long black hair for a him. And she walked like a her, clutched her jacket like a her. Dwight flicked his low beams and got out of the car. "Mornin' ma'am, you alright?"

She didn't say anything just kept coming and that dog walking right beside her, keeping his eyes on Dwight and the

5

dog's eyes shining blood red in the headlights. Dwight dropped his hand to his holster and unsnapped the hammer strap. "I sure hope that dog is friendly."

The woman's black cowboy hat was so sodden it drooped over her face, her red and black nylon jacket was molded to her shoulders like slick skin. "You the police?"

"Yes, ma'am. Bosque County sheriff's department."

When she stopped, the dog stopped too. "I thought I could take care of myself. A woman hasn't much chance against two of them."

"Yes, ma'am. You're going to catch your death standing out there, why don't you come in the car and I'll put the heater on." When he opened the door, he added, "Not the dog."

Young Dwight Blanchard spent most of his working days in his Mustang patrol car. Dwight kept a pine tree air freshener dangling from the rearview mirror, his own rattan seat pad and a trash receptacle he emptied faithfully after each shift.

"Ma'am, we can tie him to a fence and I'll take you into Meridian and we'll send the animal control officer for him when it gets light."

But the woman started off down the highway toward Meridian, just twenty miles away. Dwight jerked the Mustang into Drive and rolled up alongside the woman. "Ma'am, I got to take you in to the courthouse if you want to make a complaint, and I try to keep this car clean and, you're wet enough already, and I don't want no dirty dog in here messin' it up."

Finally, he slewed the car onto the shoulder blocking her. "Alright," he said. "But the dog gets in back."

He had to step out of the car because the prisoner compartment didn't open from the inside and the rain decided to give it a real burst and Dwight'd left his rain slicker inside. The dog jumped right in the back, scooting onto the floorboards on the far side. Before Dwight could protest, the woman slipped in too, slippery as a sack of wet laundry.

Though the rain was slinging itself at his back and working right through his uniform shirt Dwight said, politely, "Ma'am it'd be warmer for you up front where the heater is." She scooted over nearer the dog. "Yes, ma'am," Dwight sighed and got back behind the wheel. She and the dog were sopping and he turned on the defroster as moisture smudges crawled across the windshield. He radioed the courthouse and said he was coming in with a woman victim, female Caucasian, black-haired, forty or fifty. "What's your name, ma'am?"

"Penny Burkeholder. He's Hope."

He kept the defrost going, hotter than he liked, because cold wafted out of the prisoner's compartment like an open freezer on an August day.

She coughed, coughed again, and he hoped she didn't have anything he'd catch. He smelled wet cloth, wet dog.

"What happened with your truck? Did it seize up or quit kind of gradual?"

Dwight Blanchard couldn't have fixed a car if his life depended on it. The one time he decided, as an economy measure, to change his oil he'd cross-threaded the oil plug and Roy Mack had had to helicoil the threads, but like most male Americans, Dwight had a great many opinions about motors. Hell, might as well not know anything about the Dallas Cowboys or Houston Oilers.

"Oil pump," she said. "It has to be the oil pump."

Meridian is the county seat of Bosque County and has been since the county was formed. The courthouse is a blocky stone edifice. Small old-timey Texas buildings line courthouse square where lawyers and realtors have their offices. Since the boom fizzled, they'd been coming in late and taking long coffee breaks.

The rain had quit. In the eastern horizon a faint line promised that light was on its way soon.

"Here we are," Dwight said.

The woman shivered violently when a gust of knee-high wind touched her wet clothes, and the dog looked up at her. The dog worried he'd need to take over soon. When the time came the woman couldn't make decisions, the dog'd need to make them, and since he was a young dog he didn't know what those decisions might be. She stumbled on the bottom step and the dog made a sound in the back of his throat.

"Hush, Hope,"

Julio Del Flores was mopping up the communications center, sloshing steaming water out of a galvanized bucket and pushing it around with a filthy gray-black mop. Old Julio took the calls on the night shift, tended the jail, passed on messages, and cleaned up at the end of his shift. For his work he received a paycheck not quite half what Dwight, the junior deputy received, but it was good money (the Sheriff once remarked) for a Mexican.

The woman sat on the long scarred bench outside the partition, and Julio rang out his mop and vanished into the closet where they kept the emergency relief supplies, and brought a blanket and draped it over the woman's shoulders. "Thank you," she said through chattering teeth.

The dog shook himself, spattering dirty specks all over the wainscoting, and Julio raised one eyebrow. You may wish to say that an eyebrow cannot sigh, but Julio Del Flores's eyebrow did.

"Hope, lie down." With a clatter of bones the dog laid down.

In the light the woman was much younger than the deputy had thought, no more than thirty. And with her lanky black hair framing her pale face she was kind of pretty.

"Now, Mz. Burkeholder, if I could see some identification please?"

Her wallet was wet, the card folder damp and opaque and he wiped her driver's license on his knee. "Miss, it says your name is Penny Hilyer, is that correct? Ma'am?"

"I would give my life to be Penny Hilyer again," she said. She squeezed her eyes tight shut. "I am Penny Burkeholder. That's my maiden name."

"Yes, ma'am. I can take your statement or you can give it to another, uh, female."

"I don't need to make a report," the woman said. Clutching the edge of the blanket, her fingers were painfully white. "They didn't get me, though they surely tried. I never provoked 'em, I just wanted a ride. When Hope came through that window, I never saw two grown men so scared. 'Course they weren't real cowboys, just low-life show jocks. I'm cold. Could you send someone after my clothes? The camper's not locked. The lock's broke."

"Yes, ma'am. Another deputy will take care of that."

She looked up at him, studying his face. "I wouldn't have got in with 'em at all, except I saw them with Dickerson. That was at the stock show, you know. I'm not being real helpful, am I? Nothing happened. They tore my shirt and they scared heck out of me but everything turned out okay. It was creepy, that's all."

It was creepy riding down the road in their truck with the

tall one silent, nipping on a pint, and the other one, the one with the acne scarred face, talking about the Brangus-cross cow which he'd bought cheap and sold to somebody didn't know better. Talking about the herd he was going to start as soon as he had money saved up. "Montana, that's God's Country out there, Little Lady."

"How far you say it was to the all-night mechanic?"

She wouldn't have got in their truck at all but she remembered them from the Stock Show, Friday night hanging around with the other show jocks after the animals were fitted, and the trimming stands were empty, and the wash racks drying, and the radios playing in the aisles between the pens and a few people wrapped up in quilts, snoozing in empty pens, and some of the younger jocks brought in beer and talked and drank and played cards. She'd seen the acne-faced one talking to Dickerson. Dickerson used to show Angus cattle, but he was showing Chianina these days.

When her truck's oil pressure dropped right off the gauge, Penny wasn't an hour out of Fort Worth, and she switched off and coasted onto the shoulder, her headlights going yellow and dim. She'd been feeling pretty good about her new job and Hope's third place at the sheepdog trial. The second she opened the hood, she could smell the hot oil.

Her bad luck that those two stopped. She asked could they send a mechanic back from the next twenty-four hour gas station and the tall one, Marvin, said, "I'm a stranger in this part of Texas, ma'am. Maybe you should come with us and ride back with the mechanic," and she thought it was okay because she'd seen them with Dickerson. She jumped Hope into the back of their pickup where she could keep an eye on him through the sliding window. A few drops of rain hit the roof.

"I seen that dog at the show," the tall one said. "I saw you and him loading cattle. What you get for a dog like that?"

"Hope's not for sale. He isn't fully trained yet."

Then the acne-scarred one told her how he'd had a dog in Montana who'd fetch any cow he wanted out of the herd. "Just tell Shep that damned cow's name, and he'd be off like a shot."

The tall one drank from his pint and held it out to Penny.

"No thanks."

"Ain't no dog can do that, P.T." the tall one said. "They ain't so smart as that."

"You tell Marvin about those dogs, Little Lady. And don't you make no liar out of me." P.T. began to stroke Penny's leg.

"Hey," she said. "Cut that out."

"Oh, there's no harm in it," he said. "I ain't mean like Ol' Marvin."

The rain was coming down pretty good and the road sign flicked by quick as a ghost. ENTERING DEL RIO: GREEN RIVER ORDINANCE ENFORCED. "There," Penny said. "Somebody might be open."

"Nobody open until Waco," Marvin said. "I know some good mechanics in Waco."

"I thought you said you were strangers here."

"Not me. That was him. I never said nothin'. You sure you don't want a nip? Might make you friendlier."

A Gulf convenience store lighted up. "There's one," she said.

"Too late. We're past it."

In the mirror, the lighted gas station got smaller. Marvin turned the wipers to high. "I kind of like the rain," he said. "Makes things kind warm and cozylike."

"I told you," Penny said. "Take your hand off me."

11

P.T. kept his hand where it was. In a flat voice he said, "Marvin, you ever meet a girl traveling the circuit by herself wasn't a whore?"

"I don't guess I have. There was that June Lynn gal we picked up outside of Abilene, she said she wasn't no whore but she took the money when we was done. Remember, you said ten dollars and I said it was worth twenty so we left her a ten and a five and it was my ten."

P.T. kneaded Penny's breast, just went right for it. She slapped his hand and he squeezed and it hurt, it really hurt. "Don't make it rough on yourself, Little Lady. We get done and we'll leave you enough to fix that old truck of yours. Never did see a Dodge truck worth a damn anyway."

There was something so impersonal about the hand working her breast that it might have been mechanical. It was just a hand, just a breast. "No!" Penny hollered and hauled off and slugged him. Blood spouted out of his nose. He grabbed her wrists but she bucked against his hands and butted at him.

"Now you just stop that. Marvin, you're gonna have to help, you want any of this."

And Marvin pulled off the road into a picnic area and braked and got his arm around her neck and clamped down until blood spots swam in front of her eyes and P.T.'s voice got dim like it was a long way away. "Oh lookee here," he said. "She's got two of 'em." That's when her jacket tore.

With her right hand, she groped behind her head for the sliding window latch and nudged the window partway open and Hope's furry body mashed her eye into Marvin's forearm as he burled through. Hope landed on the transmission hump, spun round and his smile was one hundred percent ivory. Hope said something deep in his throat and P.T. snatched his hand back and said, "Christ, lady!"

Penny's right eye hurt. She swallowed her yelp because Hope would have misunderstood. "Hope," she gasped. "Stand!"

"Don't get nothin' started in here," P.T. said. She heard the muffled click of his door handle.

"He'll tear out your damn throat!"

Hope muttered and drops of drool landed on Marvin's pant leg. P.T. slung his door open and rolled out but Hope kept his eyes on Marvin.

Penny squinted through her left eye. "I should set him on you, tinhorn."

"Don't you do nothin' rash. A man-bitin' dog, you know what's gonna happen to that dog. They come put a bullet in that dog, you know how that goes. Dog ain't allowed to bite no man."

P.T. was dancing in front of the truck. "Put that bastard out of there."

When Penny tumbled out of the truck, she landed wrong and twisted her ankle and she called Hope and he came to her side, light and quick as a threat. She hobbled backward as P.T. scurried back in, slammed the door, and slapped the doorlock down. He fumbled through the glove compartment until he uncovered a big old pistol, which he pointed through the window. "Get away from that mutt," he said.

"Hope, get behind," and the dog faded behind her legs. Penny said, "If you shoot him, you'll have to shoot me. You ready for that?"

For a moment she thought P.T. was mad enough to do it.

She backed onto the highway and when a car came along, she waved her arms frantically, but it whooshed by.

"That's how it went," Penny told Deputy Blanchard. "After they drove off the rain got worse. I know some of those trucks saw me too, but maybe they didn't want to pick up a dog. We walked down that road for hours."

The dog sneezed and rubbed his paws over his nose. Dwight said, "We'll type up a statement for you to sign and get some pictures of your injuries so we can prove assault when we get those two in court."

"I don't want a photograph of me lookin' like this."

Dwight Blanchard stole a glance at his watch. "Ma'am, don't you want them fellows caught? You heard 'em say it. You aren't the first woman they done this to."

"You won't catch them," she said, that flat. "So there's no reason for me to have pictures made so some of your deputies can pull 'em out on a Saturday night and make jokes about how awful I look."

For the first time, Julio lifted his head from his mopping. "They not do this, I think," he said. "Nobody laughs about victims."

"I'm no victim!"

Dwight Blanchard mumbled, "Yes, ma'am," and reached behind him for the phone. "This Dickerson, fellow—how could I get hold of him?"

"Dickerson Land and Cattle, Salina, Kansas. Big man, rodeo belt buckle, chocolate-colored hat."

Dwight told the answering machine who he was and please call back in connection with a criminal investigation. To Penny he said, "You'll have to go through the ID books."

Hope lay at Penny Burkeholder's feet and felt every involuntary shiver that rippled through her. Hope smelled her cold exhaustion, knew when her head nodded forward, jerked upright again. She said, "I'd like to use your phone, please. I've got a job waiting for me down near Lampasas and I got to tell them I broke down."

"This is Oren Wright," the telephone said. "We're lambing now and I'm out in the barn . . ."

There were six scrapbook-size books on the long table, full of men's faces, old, young, none of them looking happy to be there. Some held their number placards fastidiously, some like they had a threat at their elbow, some bluffed it out. Though they could rape and kill, they looked like little boys. "Can I have a dry blanket, please?" Penny asked.

Julio went out for a platter of refried beans, rice, and tortillas in bean gravy. He brought her two small cups of tea and explained the Antler didn't have any large cups. The tea warmed her right down to her toes and she pushed the clumsy books aside to put food into her stomach with a flimsy plastic fork.

Deputy Blanchard brought her duffle bag and the news that Roy, the mechanic, had towed her truck in and was going to tear into it. "He doesn't think it's the oil pump," he said.

Dwight went home. Julio answered the phone and said the Sheriff was in Fort Worth and wouldn't be back until tomorrow night—"the Sheriff's showin' those miniature horses of his." Penny Burkeholder went to the women's room down the hall and changed into her work clothes: pale blue panties, worn Wrangler blue jeans, bra, and a flannel overshirt. She ran a comb through her hair. In the mirror she saw the gray face of a sexless, crazy woman. "Ah," she said, "the heck with it."

After nine, the courthouse filled up and people came in and out of the office for this or that. Penny turned each page in the big books. She ran her finger over the faces so she wouldn't lose where she'd been.

A long-faced quiet deputy typed Penny Burkeholder's statement and had her sign it. At eleven-thirty, Jack Dickerson called. No, he didn't know any cowboys Marvin or P.T.

"You know how it is at the Fort Worth Stock Show. There must be ten thousand people in those barns on show night and half of them are cowboys, or hope to be. What's this P.T. supposed to have done?"

"We'd just like to talk to him, Mr. Dickerson."

"Well, if you could tell me some more, maybe I could narrow it down. I don't come to the whole show, you know, just the Chianina show. I had a Reserve Champion Female this year, and if I was the judge, she was head and shoulders over the Grand. And I wasn't the only one who thought so, either. Kent Morell, of the M Bar spread outside Houston. There's no better judge of livestock than old Kent and he said my heifer was twice the animal the Grand was. What you say P.T. done?"

"Assault, he—"

"And how big a fella was he? Did he wear a Texas hat? What shape was it?

The deputy covered the phone to ask.

Penny said that P.T. had a black hat, down in front and back, you know, like a bull rider.

Jack Dickerson was awful sorry he couldn't help but there were so many cowboys and a man couldn't be expected to remember them all, but if he thought of anything he'd surely call. "I surely hope nobody got hurt?"

"She fought 'em off. She had a dog."

"Well now, that's nice. If she thinks of anything more about those fellas tried to rape her, you call me."

"Who are they?" Penny asked.

"He doesn't remember. You know how many people go through the barns at that show."

"He was talking to them like he knew them. I wouldn't have got in their truck if they didn't know Dickerson."

When Penny stood up, all the color drained out of her face and she took a sideways step to catch her balance. "Hey, you okay? You want me to call the Rescue Squad?"

Penny shook her head. "I want to find out about my truck."

Roy Mack's garage was right beside his doublewide, after the road turns to dirt just before it crosses the Brazos.

The road changed from tan to black in Roy's drive from all the crankcase oil he'd put down there to kill the dust, and the rain glistened iridescent as peacock tails in puddles beside the road.

Penny told Hope to stay in the police car and picked her way around the puddles to where her truck waited, hood up, under a tree. A tremendous limb supported a heavy block and tackle. Behind the road, the brush had grown up taller than a man. You could just see the snout of a Pontiac X37 glaring from the weeds and there was a big baker's van back in the cattails. The wrecker was about as shiny as it could get. ROY'S TOY, that's what the bug screen said, and this must be Roy coming toward her, bandy-legged, lank-haired in oily blue jeans and rolled-over cowboy boots. "This yours?" he asked without preamble. "Real trucks them old Dodges, torque won't quit. Now you take that old three eighteen and put a four speed behind it and it'll pull grannie's teeth, I got to tell you . . ."

"It is the oil pump isn't it?"

"Nope. And Lordy, just count the leaves in those rear springs; you could haul four ton back there without bottoming out. I believe you owe me fifty dollars for the tow. That's less'n you'd pay in Waco."

Penny counted through her thin sheaf of bills. "I got a check here for three hundred fifty dollars from the Southeastern Livestock Exposition—that's the Fort Worth Stock Show. It's prize money. Me and Hope won third place in the sheepdog trial there. When you can come third against Bud Boudreau and Herbert Holmes, you've done something. I don't have a bank account. I'm on the road for the present." She extended the check but he backed away from it. "Look, it's perfectly good and it'll cover the towing and the repairs and—"

"Maybe so, maybe not."

"I haven't got but forty-five dollars cash. What do you mean, maybe not?" Out in the brush were the dim shapes of other one-time-vehicles, presently refuges for small animals. "It's got to be the oil pump. I'm sure if you put a new oil pump in it I can get going again."

Wordlessly Roy bent and dragged the oil pan out from where it had laid since he unbolted it. He fished around in the muck until he came up with a slick slim arc of metal, about three inches long. "Broke ring," he said.

"Just the one?"

"I haven't puzzled that but it don't matter, you got to re-place them all. Ring sets aren't much, your money's in the time it takes to get at 'em. Easiest way is to pull the whole motor, work on it out here in the air."

18

"How much?"

He scratched his head with the tip of the broken ring. "I don't want to tell you no lies. If it's just one ring and it never scored the cylinder and the pistons are still good and you can reuse the bearings, you're looking at most of that three-hundred-fifty-dollar check. But if it scored the cylinder walls or damaged a piston it'd come to more'n the truck is worth. Me, I hate to tear down a motor and not replace the bearings anyway. New rings, bearings, and the towing. I guess I could take that check."

Penny set her neat small name on the endorsements line. She said, "I got no way of getting around."

"Lady, I don't normally keep ring sets for a 1966 Dodge 318 V8 here where I can reach for 'em."

"I got a job waiting for me outside Lampasas. They're lambing now and need an extra hand. Hundred fifty a week and a place to stay and feed for me and my dog."

"You can catch a Trailways in Waco."

"You can't take a dog on a bus."

Roy shrugged. "Put the dog in the pound. Jobs are scarcer than dogs."

"When I broke down I was just a hundred and thirty miles to Lampasas. I guess we can hitchhike."

That afternoon, Penny looked through pictures, she'd had no idea there were so many. Julio signaled to Penny to pick up the phone.

"This is Oren Wright," the voice said. "You in the sheriff's office?" The voice was young, but tired.

"Hi," Penny said. "I broke down. I busted a ring outside Meridian. I got my truck towed into town, but it'll be a while before they get to it."

"Uh-huh. Lost a set of triplets this morning, dead when I got out there. Mother hadn't even cleaned them off. I was countin' on you bein' here this mornin' so I let my part-timers take the day off." There was a long, long pause. "Sorry," he said. "It's hard to think straight when I been awake so long. Okay. Tomorrow morning I'll fetch you, I'll come myself, or I'll send one of the hands. Be on the steps of the courthouse at seven."

Two scrapbooks left. The pictures had quit being men. They were splotches and lines, numbers and shadows. It was 4:30 P.M. when she called it quits. Penny stood and stretched. Her back hurt, her eye hurt, the nape of her neck hurt. Hope stood and stretched too. He yawned. It was getting dark outside. Julio had gone home at three and his replacement, a darker Mexican, hadn't said two words. Brisk heels clicked by in the hall.

When Deputy Blanchard came back on at six, Penny asked him if he'd give her a lift to a motel and he said there was only Brice's and he'd see if they had vacancies.

Brice's didn't take dogs. They didn't allow any liquor in their rooms either but the deputy kept that information to himself.

"Why don't they allow dogs? Hope is well behaved, never makes a mess or anything."

"You hungry?"

He took her out to the Antler Cafe, Penny ate chicken fried steak and Dwight had two cups of weak coffee. Penny asked the waitress for a half pound of hamburger meat for her dog and took it outside on a paper plate and set it down for Hope. Hope waited until she went back inside before he wolfed it down. He didn't like for anyone to watch him eat.

Dwight said, "I'm sorry about the motel. There's nobody in the jail. It's free and it's clean."

The jail was upstairs in the courthouse. Dwight Blanchard piled two thin cotton mattresses on a lower bunk and covered the faded blue ticking with another army blanket. "We don't have pillow cases, I'm afraid."

Penny sat on the bunk, on the very end of it.

"If we pick up anybody, drunk or anything, I'll tell the jailer to put them in the far cell. Look, I'm sorry." He swung the door back and forth to show it wasn't locked. "You want anything, just come outside and ask. Anything, coffee or anything."

The windows were covered with wire mesh, painted and repainted so half their thickness was paint. The wall was splotched where the jailers had painted over graffiti. Outside, a pickup truck paused before making the turn. Two young lovers pressed together on the driver's side. No one ever sits quite that close again.

At Penny's feet Hope lay with his dark head on his paws. Penny said, "Hope, I don't know how long I can go on."

Hope raised his big head. His eyes were pools of light. "It is not thy fault," Hope said.

"Fat lot of comfort you are."

AT SEVEN SHARP, she was waiting on the courthouse steps, duffle on one side and dog on the other. She looked at Oren Wright for a minute before she slung her duffle. "Took you long enough," she said.

"I didn't expect to be makin' this trip at all."

She tossed her duffle into the back.

Oren stepped out, stretched, inspected the sky. It was supposed to be warmer today, sixty. No more rain. The sky was very big and streaked with red from the sunrise. Haze muted the rim where the sky met the horizon. "You drive a stick shift?"

The dog jumped in and scooted over the hump to the passenger side. "He'll ride under your feet," she said. "He won't bother you none."

"How 'bout the back?"

"I don't like to ride him in back unless I have to." She eyed the 1976 Toyota minitruck. "He's worth twice what this truck is."

Oren rotated his shoulders in their sockets, ran right up against that twinge from the old bucking horse injury. "Don't suppose he can hurt anything," he said. "Take 6 to 281 south to Lampasas. Wake me at the feed store." Oren worked his feet around the dog and tugged his hat down over his eyes.

Penny tried the brakes, which went a long way toward the floorboards before they grabbed. She clunked the four speed in gear. "Hope you got new rings in this thing," she said as they pulled away trailing a cloud of blue smoke.

He tugged his hat lower.

Penny Burkeholder was twenty-six years old last June fifteenth. She figured her new boss to be about the same. He was one of those long-muscled, small-buttocked, wiry cowboys who stay that way all their life, developing a modest paunch over their belt buckles in middle age. Like whippets they aren't much for stamina but they are pure hell for speed. He hadn't shaved for a couple days. His hair was bleached out, dented around his head by his hat. Blue jeans, gabardine shirt, runover boots: that's what there was of him, 165 pounds wet. He lolled against the door and Penny hoped he'd locked the damn thing. Way her luck was running, it'd be average if her new boss toppled out onto Texas 281 and left her, unemployed, with all the explaining to do.

Rolling along, one arm on the window, Penny Burkeholder daydreamed. Fort Worth Stock Show had been the same as all the other stock shows except bigger. The arena where they had the sheepdog trial had high walls and metal trusses overhead. It was painted white and the railings were red and the rows of plastic seats were blue. From the trusses hung flags of the United States and Texas, side by side, neither an inch bigger than the other.

She walked right by the table where the judge sat and he touched the brim of his cap and said, "Good luck, honey," and her mouth was so dry she hadn't been able to respond.

Hope was an eighteen-month-old smooth-coated Border Collie mostly black and white but smudges of brown on his legs and nose. He was a blocky dog, 40 pounds, strong shouldered and calm. At a trial, he must fetch the sheep, drive them through obstacles, put them in a pen and, finally, separate one sheep from the others. Trials are trickier than that, but that's what happens, more or less, in that order.

Eight minutes later, Penny walked off past the judge and he asked, "What's the breeding on that dog?" And Penny said he was by Nop, out of Florence Wilson's Kate and the judge said, well he sure does know how to listen.

Most stores in Lampasas had wooden awnings for shade, but Lampasas Seeds and Feeds was a rough clapboard mill building down by the railroad tracks, no shade anywhere.

When Penny shoved her boss's shoulder he opened one bleary eye. He got out of the truck, said, "I won't be long," and disappeared inside.

Penny and Hope went around back. While Hope relieved himself, Penny looked away. Hope didn't like anybody watching him while he did his business. He was funny that way.

The pale sun didn't have very much warmth but it was warmer than Virginia.

Oren set a box of vet supplies in the bed, wedged it against her duffle. On the outskirts of town, he stopped at a modest shack on the lot of a mini shopping mall. "Hope you like Mexican," he said.

Wonderful aromas rose from the greasy sack he set on the seat between them.

"Tamales. Just unpeel 'em out of the husk. There's napkins on top."

They were hot and cornmealy and full of meat. Hope didn't beg or anything but he hadn't eaten since last night, so Penny passed him four tamales, which he delicately nibbled to her fingertips.

Outside Lampasas, the road narrowed and turned to gravel and Oren bumped across a ditch, and lifted a wire gate. "This is the Bar Kay Ranch," he said. "Place I rent is out back."

The tamales were good but they were greasy and Penny was dabbing at her lips with a paper napkin when they drove into the barnyard. There wasn't much to it: barn, corral, couple pickups, gas tank, tiny travel trailer, and a cowboy chasing a sheep and not catching it.

Since the sheep had a half-born lamb dangling out of it and since the lamb was flopping up and down, the cowboy chasing the sheep wasn't as funny as he might of been, even when he made a dive and went headlong. Half his face, half his pants, half his shirt, became stinking black mud. The ewe had joined a dozen others in the corner of the corral. The lamb dropped on the ground and, spooked, Mama hurried away.

"Hope," Penny said. When Hope came out of the truck, Penny waited until he was looking at the right sheep before she said, "That one."

Hope saw a crowd of woolies, smelled the lambing scent, the powerful stink of blood and mucus, swept around the far side of the corral and dropped down on his elbows to scoot under the rails where the stunned, bewildered new mother saw him and stamped her foot. Faced by this predator, she remembered her lamb, rushed back, and stood over it protectively.

The dog retreated a pace, and the ewe fell to cleaning the mucus off her new baby. Hope laid down as the mother cleaned, stomped, nickered, returned to the exciting thing that was her own, _hers!_

The cowboy paused at the spigot to wash the muck off his hands. Close up, Penny could see he had mud in his long lank hair. "God damn these sheep," he said.

"You're fired," Oren said.

"Too late," the cowboy said and got in his truck and gunned it. Another cowboy, younger, came out of the trailer with a cup in his hand. He raised a hand in a lackadaisical salute and scratched his butt against the doorpost.

"Where's Lonnie goin'?" he asked. The cowboy was nineteen or twenty and his jeans hung off his skinny butt. "I ain't gonna do all the work myself," he said.

Inside the corral, the new mother looked up at the sky, surprised as a fresh contraction shook her.

"She's got another one," Penny said. "You got pens?"

The young cowboy said, "I don't know we got any clean ones. Lonnie was going to do that."

Oren shook his head tiredly and led Penny into the long, metal pole barn. "Used to be horses," he said. "We tore out the stall dividers and kept the tack room for supplies. You can bunk here."

The tack room was a stall with a concrete floor, dusty high window, a refrigerator (into which Oren put medicines), and an army cot with a mattress, a couple Hudson Bay blankets, and pillow. Oren looked dubious. "You sure you can do with this?"

"Last night I slept in jail." She set her duffle on the bed. "Show me your operation."

As Oren toured her through the barn, past the pens of ewes and lambs, the young cowboy started forking used bedding from vacated pens. Oren told Penny about the shots and docking, what to feed the ewes, and where feed was kept. Each four-by-four wooden pen had a metal card holder where special instructions were written for the next man on shift.

"You got twenty-six hundred ewes? How many of us is there?"

With a thumb, Oren Wright jabbed her, him, and the cowboy. "I got to get some shut-eye or I won't be no account for nothing. Can you handle it until night?"

"I expect. These ewes the only ones bagged up?"

He shook his head. "They're the ones we could catch. We got newborns out in the breaks, some a week old never had their shots."

When Oren Wright left, the young cowboy rolled a cigarette. "Where you from?" he asked.

"Somewhere the help don't quit as soon as the boss walks out the door. I'm gonna need a dozen clean pens."

The lambing barn had four rows of pens against the long walls and back-to-back in the middle. At any one time the pens could hold eighty ewes and their lambs. When things went well, a ewe came into the barn on Monday and left on Thursday, and after her apartment was renovated the shepherd could install a newcomer. When a ewe had trouble—mastitis, milk fever, pneumonia, blue bag—the pens filled with sick sheep and the sheep housing stock shrank. Penny spent a couple hours examining the ewes in the barn, medicating those that needed it, turning others with their lambs out into the sunshine. She slipped bands on lambs' tails, checked new mothers for milk supply, milked out ewes for their colostrum, ear notched bad mothers so they could be culled. Hope found himself a straw bale and laid down with his head on his paws.

The young cowboy didn't say another word but kept at the pens making room for new arrivals. At noon Penny got cold tamales out of Oren's truck. She ate four, Hope ate four.

"The main flock—the flock with the untreated lambs, which direction are they?"

The cowboy pointed at the expanse of broken hills and ravines behind the ranch.

Penny said, "Come by, Hope. OUT." And the dog shot off. Penny returned to the barn then to gather used syringes and needles to boil on her hotplate.

"Where's he goin'?" the cowboy asked as Hope climbed the first ridge and disappeared in the mesquite.

"After the sheep."

"How's he know where to go?"

Penny dropped needles into her boiling water.

"He just does, that's all."

Hope set out on his gather with joy in his heart. This is what he was always meant to do, nothing less: to seek woolies and bring them home.

The pasture was 280 acres of rough scrub, more mesquite than grass. Plenty of woolie sign, scraps of wool clinging to the thorn bushes, but Hope went out, a half mile, three quarters of a mile until one woolie saw him and bolted inward for safety and company. Hope paused, was this all? Not all, he decided and swung out again seeking more. The second band was much larger and spooky. The moment they saw him they were away, shooting off to his right, but Hope didn't pursue them directly, he kept on going. When he stopped he was a mile from where he'd started and all the bands of sheep were between him and Penny.

Penny went through the refrigerator combining half-empty vials, tossing empties, making a list of what she had and what she needed. Strong iodine, neomycin, boluses, covexin 8. . .

"That dog of yours done took off, huh?" The cowboy was leaning against the door of the tack room.

"This is my room," she said. "Off limits."

"Ain't we particular," he said but he did take a step backward."

"You gonna get the feed out for those sheep or you gonna stand around jawing?"

The tack room door dragged when Penny pulled it closed. She put a fresh pot of water on the hot plate and watched the elements turn red. She wondered how many women there were like her, runaways or in hiding. The mug she rinsed said TEXAS AGGIES.

Out in the pasture, Hope was combining the flocks. Ewes get hysterical if their new lamb gets separated, which happens if the sheep are brought along too fast. When a ewe loses track of her lamb she'll rush back to the spot she last saw it and only a dog's teeth can stop her. Beyond a point—and a dog's teeth bring that point on promptly—ewes lose what small sense they customarily possess and go insane rushing hither and yon, no rhyme or reason, uncontrollable.

So Hope stayed back, just far enough to make the ewes uneasy so they'd slide along at a walk, their lambs beside them.

He slipped beneath low mesquite bushes, light and shadow, and the sheep drifted away nervously.

That strange smell coming out of that burrow? Hope had never smelled armadillo before—he'd maybe come back later. He haunted the flock of sheep, a presence in their rear, more sensed than seen, ghosting through the brush. The sheep streamed over the brow of the hillock behind Oren Wright's barn, like a thick, bumpy liquid.

"Well, I be damned," the young cowboy said.

"We got enough pens for these critters?"

"Yes, ma'am. Yes, ma'am."

At midnight, the alarm went off in Oren Wright's trailer and he sat up and wondered briefly where he was. He splashed water on his face, thought he'd shave, maybe later. He'd slept in his shorts and socks and now he slipped into the dirty insulated coveralls that hung by the door and pushed his feet into his calf-high rubber boots. He was out the door under the brilliant wash of stars before he remembered to be worried: what if that girl wasn't what she'd seemed?

He'd met her at the Fort Worth Stock Show. Oren had raised and showed sheep since he was a boy of nine, first with the 4-H and later with the FFA. Oren brought his show sheep into the stock show barn five minutes before the deadline and trimmed them in the barn. He hadn't had time to do any fancy work at home. He combed and clipped his animals, making not-quite-perfect animals look perfect. At night he slept in an empty stall, right next to them. Plenty of sheepmen paused to look over his best ram lamb after the judge (from Brigham Young University) gave Oren the blue ribbon for senior ram lamb and light purple for reserve champion Rambouillet. It wasn't much prize money: his blue ribbon was worth a hundred bucks but the purple ribbon brought $250 and a fellow from Kerrsville said he liked the looks of the ram lamb. Could he call him with an offer?

"Sure. I'm lambing right now so you'll probably get the machine."

Lamb prices had been off, so Oren was scraping hard to make his feed payments. The prize money was unbudgeted and a pleasure. At the Budweiser stand he bought himself a two-dollar-and-fifty-cent cup of beer. He was done with his part of the showing but, according to the rules, couldn't remove his animals until all the sheep classes were finished, so he hung both ribbons over his pens beside the sign that said: OREN WRIGHT, LAMPASAS, TX. GRADE AND REGISTERED RAMBOUILLETS.

Rodeo tickets were sold out so he watched the miniature-horse show. Costumed owners brought out their stallions "under thirty-six inches in height" and stood the feisty little beasts for the judge's inspection. Country people have strange ideas of fun.

After the last stallion pranced out of the arena, they brought out pens and slatted gates for the sheepdog trial. Oren'd seen working dogs before but never a trial, and he sat, sipping his beer, kind of entranced by it all. The checks in his breast pocket made his pocket feel warm.

That's what he needed for his sheep, a good dog. But where in the world would he find the time to train it? He didn't watch the entire trial, but he did see Penny run with Hope and he liked the confidence the young dog showed.

A couple hours later, he'd seen the Budweiser Clydesdales, seen the llamas, walked through the poultry barn (when he was in 4-H, he'd also shown chickens), and eaten two hot dogs. Penny was carding out montadale ewes. "That's a nice dog you got there," Oren said.

"If I'd been a little quicker at the gate we might have taken second. Wasn't Hope's fault."

"How'd you learn how to do it?"

"My daddy is Lewis Burkeholder . . . " She paused like she expected Oren to know him. "It's a hobby of his, the sheepdogs. He has that Nop dog, maybe you've heard of him?"

"First sheepdog trial I ever saw was tonight." He offered his hand for the dog to sniff but the dog ignored him. "You grow up with stock?"

She said she'd gone away to Ohio State Ag School and majored in sheep management, but she'd been away from it for a couple of years and was starting over. "Me and Hope are on the trial circuit this year, first time for both of us. I am completely determined to run in the National Finals this year"— she gestured at her grooming tools: comb, clippers, wool whitener—"so I'll do whatever sheep work comes along."

With that check burning up his breast pocket Oren asked her, casual as he could, if she'd ever lambed out sheep before. He said, "I been lookin' for somebody on my place . . . "

When Penny hadn't showed up, he'd been annoyed but not surprised; wouldn't be the first farmhand to give work a pass. When she phoned and asked him to pick her up at the Bosque County Courthouse, that hadn't been anything new either, except that she was a woman. He'd been so tired and his two cowboys didn't like sheep and wouldn't learn the simplest things about them. They didn't know much about cows either but could distinguish between dozens of pickup option packages. So Oren fetched her and fell into the longest uninterrupted sleep he'd managed since lambing began.

THE SHEEP BARN WAS CALM, one ewe nickering to her lamb. Penny had a newborn in her arms, banding its tail. There were many, many ewes in pens, most with older lambs.

"Hope brought 'em in. Hold this iodine will you?"

"Some of those lambs are two weeks old."

"I figured we'd keep 'em in one night, figure who was who, see if there's any of these ewes need culling. You can put them out in the morning."

She set the lamb gently back in the pen. "Okay, Sonny, here's your mama," and gave him a little push. "When you want me in the morning?"

He told her ten sharp and she said okay, give her door a kick about eight and could she borrow the pickup to go into town and get some groceries and was there a laundromat?

He said, "I'll pay for the groceries. That was part of the deal."

She said, "Hope's dog food too. You're getting his work thrown in for free. I reckon you can feed him."

Everything was so quiet in the barn, ewes snoozing or nursing, lambs banked up next to their moms. It was that quiet that blocked Oren's rejoinder. For the first time in weeks, his animals were content. The woman pulled off her manure-filthy boots outside her room and summoned the dog and closed the door behind them, and Oren could have sworn he heard two people talking together in there.

Penny chose to herd sheep. Hope had that choice made for him two centuries ago. Hope's many times removed great-granddam was a bitch named Fly. Fly looked quite a bit like Hope, and if you could set the two dogs side by side, you'd remark the similarity. Fly was smaller than Hope but had a much thicker coat. She was a harder beast than Hope, quicker with her teeth. She lived long before the first sheepdog trials, during a lean and hungry time in Scotland.

Fly belonged to shepherd Jock MacRae, who tended sheep in Glen Lyons on land that had once belonged to the Campbells but belonged now to Sir Isaac Belevedere, who had served as colonel of artillery under the Duke of Cumberland at Culloden and used the slaughter after that battle to improve his family fortunes. This says little about Jock's bitch Fly but helps to explain why her master tended another man's beasts on ground he'd once worked as a free crofter. Why Jock and Fly slept in a filthy stone bothy and why the smoke of Jock's fires exited through the broken front door.

One night in late summer, Fly came into season and Jock bred her to a neighboring shepherd's dog, Luath by name. As the days cooled and shortened, Jock and Fly climbed the great hill through the lowering mists into the sunlight where harrier hawks and eaglets soared and Cheviot sheep browsed in this brilliant air. In the distance, other hills poked through the mists, which Jock knew to be tended by men like him and dogs like Fly.

In September of that year, Jock took Sir Isaac's lambs to the market at Sterling. The drove roads Jock and Fly traveled shunned the towns, crossed high passes, meandered beside still waters, and one flock followed another with no more space between them than prevented intermingling. The shepherd traveled at the rear of his flock, depending on his dog to range ahead, prevent wrong turns, retrieve ewes inclined to straying. "She was such a thrifty bitch," Jock said later, "I never suspected a thing."

They were on the Grampian downgrade, four hours east of Sterling, when Fly dropped her first pup. So near the town, every hundred yards presented a new lane to tempt the ewes, and Fly raced forward to check escape, raced to the rear to chivvy laggards, and as each pup came, she bruskly cleaned it and laid it in a safe spot, beside a milepost, perhaps or just inside a gorse thicket where it wouldn't come to harm.

Jock noted this but his duty was plain: to bring his master's lambs to Sterling and turn them over to Sir Isaac's factor. Only after Sir Isaac's factor closed the gate on the lambs, marked the final tally in his book, and said, "That'll be right," did Jock turn to Fly and say, "That'll do, Lass," and the bitch shot off, back the way she'd come.

A half hour later, Jock was having a pint at the Black Bull Arms when the bitch dashed in, dropped a pup at his feet and was gone again. Jock told the other shepherds how she'd had her pups and abandoned them to continue her work and they said, "Aye" and "Ah then."

When Fly reappeared with her second pup, Jock was eating a great chunk of cheese. Men smoked their pipes, discussed the

terrible price of fat lambs, the progress of British arms and Old
Boney. Fly brought her third pup and paused, panting, to let
them suck. By the time she returned with the fourth pup, the
landlord had found a topless cask and bedded it with rags where
the pups could nestle. Each pup she went for was farther back
along the road and she dashed through oncoming flocks, duck-
ing the curses and stones of drovers whose animals she af-
frighted. The next pup was dead and Fly's feet were bloody
from travel. The final pup was dead too, but she laid him beside
his dead brother before she clambered into the cask. No shepherd remarked at the time about what he'd seen, but before he
left Sterling the next morning, Jock had promised every one
of the pups, and Sir Isaac's factor himself found space behind
the seat of his ponycart for the bitch and her brood. Jock, of
course, walked.

THAT IS WHAT Hope was—his ancestors: Fly; Spot; Nell;
Corrie, who died trying to bring her flock to shelter in a March
blizzard; Wiston Cap, who won the International Sheepdog
Trial when he was only two years old; Nop, who'd been the
finest sheepdog in America.

When Penny pulled off her boots and went inside with
Hope, her shoulders hurt and her feet were wrinkly from the
rubber boots and her hand throbbed where she'd punched a
ewe. She picked up Hope's empty bowl and opened a can of
Old El Paso refried beans for herself. Her walls were painted
plywood, her floor was concrete, but so long as Hope lay beside her cot, his head on his paws, this room was home.

"I lost my temper with that spotty-faced ewe," she con-
fessed.

"Woolies cannot help what they do," Hope said.

"Yeah, but I can't stand it when a ewe won't mother her lamb. That poor little lamb don't want anything but mother's milk and when the ewe starts butting him away, deliberately starving it . . ."

"It is not thy child," Hope said.

"I thought I told you not to talk about that!" Sometimes Hope could jolly her out of her grieving by acting the silly pup, but the only sure cure was work. Their work was fulfillment of Hope's deepest impulses and forgetfulness for her. "Tell me again about the National Finals," Hope said.

She squeezed her tea bag into her cup. "Well, Hopey, it's just the biggest, toughest trial in the whole country, that's all. You can't even enter unless you're in the top ten percent of all the open dogs in the country. . . ."

He licked his feet clean. "If I am handled correctly . . ."

"I'm not so bad!"

"Thy commands come late or too soon and thee fail to read thy sheep."

Her weariness slipped from her shoulders as Penny allowed herself to be drawn into the dog's hard Calvinist heritage where, so long as the work made sense, life made sense, and outside the work, everything was death and sorrow and swirling blackness.

IN THE MORNING Penny drove into Lampasas and returned ten to ten with her washed clothes in a blue plastic bag, cans of beef stew and ravioli, instant coffee, and the soups and spaghetti Oren had requested. "I suppose you couldn't have found a more expensive dog food." He inspected the receipt. "Sometimes they have this dog food down at the feed mill, Old Chum Dog Food, they call it."

The woman put one hand on her hip. She said, "I figured me and Hope would go out and check the sheep."

"Sure," he said. "Okay."

The cowboy, Jerry, came on at ten and stayed until eight at night. He'd been hired to do everything the girl was doing, but Jerry had no knack for the work. Jerry forgot: forgot to check the ewe's milk so the newborn wouldn't starve, forgot to make sure the lambs were nursing. Jerry mixed up ewes and lambs so nobody knew who belonged to who. Now Jerry did the simple feeding and cleaned the pens and went for bed straw when they needed it and did any small errands. By week's end he was following the woman around. "How do you do this? How do you do that?"

Every morning, Penny checked ewes with lambs and penned those who'd lambed after the morning feeding. About ten o'clock she walked out into the mesquite with Hope and eleven o'clock she'd reappear with ewes and newborns. When Jerry wanted to accompany her, she said, "Not this time, Jerry. This is the only private time Hope and me got."

February second, there was a message on the answering machine, "This is Roy Mack in Meridian, your truck is ready, it weren't nothing but the rings." Jerry volunteered to drive her but his boss said he'd do it.

The pistons were alright and the cylinder walls and Roy Mack gave her twenty dollars in change and a list of parts he'd put in. She said she didn't care about that but he gave her the list anyway.

Following her back home, Oren prepared a speech in his mind: how he'd started out with nothing, his father dead when he was eight and his mother working as a bookkeeper at the oil company to keep her three kids fed and clothed, how his high school pals had been wild but he hadn't, he'd stuck to the books, rented a place outside of town, just a shed with ten acres to keep his show flock, how he'd felt when he won his first blue ribbon, how he'd felt when, two months later, a pack of neighboring dogs got into his sheep and killed five outright, crippled three so they had to be destroyed. He'd only made it through two years of college and he knew things didn't look like much right now, but the sheep were more'n half paid for, and even in a tough year with lambs bringing forty-eight cents, he'd make enough to pay his ground rent and in a good year, he could add to his flock and maybe make a down payment on his own place. Soon as they got home he confronted her. "I was hoping we'd get a chance to talk."

She said, "It's my shift. Me and Hope got to go look at the sheep."

"We can wait a minute."

"Mr. Wright, you didn't hire me to talk." And a minute later she was chewing out Jerry for something or other and Oren went inside his trailer and watched "The Young and the Restless" on TV.

The lambs came fifty, a hundred a day. When it rained or sleeted or the wind blew, the ewes found hiding places in the mesquite and lambed there. The girl bought a new yellow slicker. Friday mornings she went into town for laundry and groceries. One bitter morning when an icy rain was coating the chapparal with diamonds, Oren Wright said, "You don't have to go out there today."

She tugged her hat down on her head and said, "If I don't, some'll die. Hope."

Michigan State Number Ninety went into labor, daybreak Tuesday morning. Number Ninety was a big strong ewe, and the contractions racked her, hoof to poll. She grunted and moaned. When Oren stooped to check her vagina, he couldn't see a thing, neither lamb hoof nor nose nor tail, so he got the surgical soap and the disposable gloves and went inside her.

Number Ninety's sire had been champion of the National Ram Show, the ram its owner had turned down four thousand dollars for. The ewe lifted her head off the ground in an arch of pain and bleated protest. She licked her lips, strained again. She was a strong ewe and Oren could give her more time to labor, so he returned to the barn and turned lambs and their mothers out into the sunlight. It was a pretty nice day, cool. It had rained last night and the lots were muddy. The tack room door opened and Hope stepped outside, stretched, yawned, looked at Oren and went outside to do his business. The woman was clattering around in there, boiling water for her morning cup of tea. Hope returned and pawed the door, once, politely to be let in.

After a bit the two of them stepped into the barn, her with her mug of steaming tea. "Mornin'."

"Uh, there's a purebred out there having trouble. Mornin'. Hope you slept well."

"That big ewe? Number Ninety? How long?"

"Sunrise, I figure." He looked at his watch for no particular reason.

She frowned. "Don't you think you better go inside? My daddy used to tell me: two hours then you take a look."

"Your daddy never had Rambouillets! I been inside her," he said. "She's dilated enough to have a lamb."

"Uh-huh." She slung a dark green rubberized tarp over her

arm. Kneeling behind the ewe, the woman went inside, against the ewe's groans and labors, to her elbow now, grimacing every time the ewe pushed against her. "There's a single in the canal," she said. "He's enormous."

Penny managed to tug one lamb foot out, then the nose; and that was that. They rolled the ewe onto her other side, tried to slip one of the lamb's shoulders past the pelvic girdle. Penny braced her feet against the sheep's rear and pulled until she couldn't pull more without pulling the leg off. Despite the tarp, her jeans were wet with blood and amniotic fluid. "Here," she said, "you try. My hand's getting cramped up."

And so the man tried too, for another half an hour, trying to slip that enormous lamb past the too small cervix. They laid a bale of straw on the mud and propped the ewe's rear end in the air and by the time that failed, the ewe's labors had nearly ceased, the lamb's tongue was turning black, and the rubber tarp was more under the mud than on top of it. The woman peeled off her surgical glove and tossed it with the previously discarded others. "Is there a good sheep vet in Lampasas?"

"Nope."

"Should we do a Caesarian?"

"This damn ewe cost me five hundred dollars!"

"Yeah. It's her dead or her and the lamb dead. You're the boss."

The ewe lay on the tarp, on her side, mouth open, ribs heaving.

"Okay, damn it." He went into the trailer and brought a .22 rifle. When Hope saw the gun he took off for the barn and didn't stop until he'd pawed open the tack room door and scooted under the bed. When the shot came, Hope faced away from the door. At the second shot, he whimpered protest.

Oren said, "Pull her onto her back, won't you? I can't work this way."

With the ewe shot, the blood supply stopped surging through the umbilical cord, and unless they moved quickly, the lamb would die. Oren's knife dented her pale pink belly, slipped under the outer skin, peeled that back, then a quick slash at the grainy white stomach muscles and they parted and inside were glistening separate packages: rumen, the ewe's seven stomachs, her guts, one big lamb, wrapped in a transparent wrap.

"Careful, don't cut the lamb."

And he laid the knife against the uterus, cut and dragged the too-big lamb out of the mother's steaming insides, those marvelous insides now useless. Penny scooped the mucus off the lamb's face and swung it by the heels, and then she laid it down on a dry patch of tarp beside its mother. The little ribs lifted once, twice.

The lamb struggled and lifted its long ears and flapped them dry and, squeakily, tried a "baa."

At that, the mother lifted her bloody head and looked at her lamb through her golden flecked eyes and nickered once, to welcome it into the world and struggled to sit upright, but couldn't, and died.

"I shot her twice," Oren said. "I would have swore she was dead."

"Yeah," Penny said. The rest of the sheep were eating hay. In the distance a hawk soared over the mesquite searching for prey.

He went to his trailer and put the gun in the closet and rinsed the blood off the knife and washed his hands and went to the barn feeling weak in the knees and took the tea she

41

handed him, which was Red Rose tea in a chipped mug but tasted pretty good. Hope came out of the tack room and thumped his tail: no more shooting, please?

"Doesn't it bother you?" he said.

Her shirt was muddy and streaked and she had a blood smudge above her left eye. "It's a mother's job to die for their young. That's what mothers do. Mother won't die for her baby isn't worth a damn in this world or the next."

February 26, Kerrville, Texas
Judge: Red Oliver, Caldwell, Texas

34 Open dogs went to the post

1. Ransome Barlow	Bute	89
2. Orin Barnes	Sioux	88
3. Herbert Holmes	Dave	87
4. Francis Raley	Dell	86
5. Penny Burkeholder	Hope	80

AS THE PENS EMPTIED of newborns, Penny moved in ewes who were having troubles. Even so, Oren started breaking down pens, one row, then two. After a week, only a dozen ewes remained in the barn and the two shepherds took a few minutes every day to clamber in the pens, palpate udders, give shots. Hope lay in the doorway of the tackroom, bored.

"How long you been here?"

"Thirty-five days."

"Seems longer than that. Look, I got a ram lamb to deliver over to Kerrville. I know they got some kind of dog trial there, part of the mohair show."

The road from Lampasas to Kerrville passes through some

43

of the prettiest country in Texas, and the hills are lush in the winter when the creeks are running and small lakes are full.

"I thought Texas would be flat," she said.

He said in some parts it was, in other parts it wasn't, how the coast near Galveston was different from the coast near Corpus Christie, how the hill country was where people bought retirement homes and ranches, at least they did during the boom, and he pointed out several closed banks—fine red marble, drive-in teller booths and all for sale. "You ain't very interested in this," he said.

"Sure I am," she said. "This trial, will any of the big handlers be there?"

Fredericksburg was settled by a particularly tidy bunch of Germans. Stone houses and neatly mowed lawns. When they stopped for breakfast, Oren ordered sausages and fried eggs. She ate a bowl of cereal. When he went for the check, she said, "I'll pay for my own. I don't want to be beholden."

He said, "If anything, I'm beholden to you. I never had a lambing go so smooth. You and that dog took the kinks right out of it."

The National Mohair Show and Shearing Contest was held outside Kerrsville in the ag expo building—a metal building with a stage inside. Young goats were pushed up to the shearing platform by 4-H boys, who kept them coming for the shearer, whose clippers flashed while another 4-H boy arm-loaded fine silky fleece into a deep burlap bag.

There were crafts booths and exhibits. One booth sold 100 percent mohair blankets. Another stall had a slick photograph of goats and fashion clothes and advised: MOHAIR: YOUR PROFIT OPPORTUNITY. A photo blowup introduced goat raisers to the

1985 Mohair Queen who grew up right here in Texas and now adorned fashion spreads in *Vogue* and *Harper's Bazaar.*

Most of the men and women wandering through the displays wore ranch clothing; blue jeans were popular, also Texas hats. Nobody wore mohair.

The trial field was out back. That's where Penny met Ethel Harwood. If she'd known Ethel was going to be here, she wouldn't have come. Ethel was an old family friend. Last thing in the world Penny wanted, right now, was old family friends.

"Honey," Ethel said. "I heard. I am so darn sorry." Penny bent over Hope where she could squeeze her dripping eyes shut, clamp them tight. She said, "This is my Hope dog."

Hope whined.

Penny touched Hope's shoulder. His hair was so slick, so coarse, and his hard muscle lay close under the skin. Penny wiped her sleeve across her face. So long as she had Hope to touch, she'd be okay. "I can't talk about it," Penny said. "I can't. This Hope dog is out of Nop. He wants to go to the Finals."

Ethel didn't quite touch Penny. "I came down for the winter Olympics, though I didn't get anything to show for it. Honey, sometimes I wonder about these darn dog trials. Go halfway across the country for ten minutes on a trial course and then don't do good. I'm getting too old for this racket."

Penny had a grip on herself and her breathing had steadied. "Who won the Olympics?" she asked.

"Young fellow name of Ransome Barlow. This is only his second year on the circuit, but he's lighting it up. Won Edgeworth last fall, and Tennessee. Second in the Finals. That Bute dog of his is a brute, and I don't think I could handle him. That's Ransome over there."

Blue jeans, dark shirt buttoned up to the neck, black hair like maybe he had some Indian blood in him. He had one boot perched on a truck bumper as he watched the dogs.

"He's not a talkative cuss, and when his run goes bad, you better not come near him, but he does know how to handle a dog. Honey, I got hot water for tea or coffee in my camper. It's that blue and cream Winnebago. And you're welcome to go in and use the john or take a nap or . . ."

But as she spoke, the girl was drifting away, insubstantial as mist, her and her dog.

For thirty years Ethel Harwood and her husband, Fred, raised the finest quarterhorses in Colorado. By 1980, when Fred died, they were selling more horses to movie stars and hobbyists than working ranchers. The money was terrific, but most of the fun had gone and Ethel was glad to let her son take over the business while she went on the road with her sheepdogs. She bought her dogs ready trained, never kept more than four, and since she wouldn't sell the dogs that didn't win trials, she didn't win many trials. In her commodious and friendly motor home, she spent nine months of the year on the road and knew everybody. She'd once offered Lewis Burkeholder $5,000 for his Nop dog. When Penny approached Ransome Barlow, Ethel shook her head, Oh dear.

Penny said, "I never worked goats before. What should I know?"

"They don't flock good. They shed easier than sheep."

"I hear you won the Winter Olympics. Congratulations."

He kept his eyes on the course. "Who are you?"

"Penny Burkeholder. From Virginia."

46

"You kin to Lewis Burkeholder? That Nop dog?"

"My daddy."

"You must be the one won the Bluegrass eight, nine years ago with some crippled-up dog."

"The Stink Dog, she—"

"That was a piece of luck." He walked to the other side of the truck, refolded his arms, and went back to watching.

Penny Burkeholder got a nice plaque for her fifth place and an envelope with forty dollars in cash. Ransome Barlow was stuffing his first-place money in his wallet when Penny said, "I thought goats were easy to shed."

"They are. You didn't ask about _keepin'_ 'em shed."

Oren Wright told her it was tough luck at the shed but he'd sure enjoyed her run, enjoyed the whole day, in fact. The FFA kids were throwing a banquet and there'd be a dance. Oren asked Penny did she know the cotton-eyed Joe? That was a real Texas dance.

Penny said she wanted to get back to Lampasas and pack, the lambing was finished, there was no more reason for her to stay in Texas.

He said he didn't know about that, there was always work on a ranch and he'd got kind of used to having her around.

"Oren," she said, "If I was looking for a man, I'd probably give you a whirl. I got no room in my heart for anyone but this dog."

SOUTHERN ARIZONA INTERNATIONAL LIVESTOCK ASSOCIATION
(SAILA) SHEEPDOG TRIAL

—— ⟡ ——

March 3, 1st go-round, Tuscon, Arizona
Judge: Bill Berhow, Lavina, Montana

62 Open dogs went to the post

1. Ransome Barlow	Bute	94
2. Betty Maddux	Mirk	89
3. Roger Schroeder	Don	88
4. Ted Johnson	Craig	86
5. Sandra Milberg	Val	83

THE WINNEBAGO WAYFARER that Beverly and Lewis Burkeholder had fixed up last summer sat under the roof in the hay shed and the barn pigeons perched on the air conditioner and cooed. The windows were dusty and the bright colors of the checked curtains Beverly had sewn (she would have been the first to tell you she was no seamstress) had faded. The sign Mark had fastened beside the door when everybody thought they'd start taking it a little easier, not retiring exactly but leaving most of the farm work to Mark and Penny, that sign— WELCOME TO OUR ROLLING HOME—had faded too.

Nop inspected the tires. Though he smelled no dog sign

48

but his own, he freshened his mark. His snout was streaked with gray and, first thing in the morning, his joints ached, but his eyes were clear and last summer, he'd come in second at the Mason Dixon trial. Lewis had retired Nop then, saying that Nop was getting past it and the trophies he'd won were enough for one dog. Nop was indifferent to trophies. If the work went well and Lewis was pleased, Nop was pleased too. Sometimes, not very often, he and Lewis would get it just right and Nop knew they were beautiful then and those were the days—not very many—he carried in his memory.

Lewis had built a traveling shelf over the driver's seat of the motor home where Nop and Hope were to have traveled, but things hadn't turned out: Mark and baby Lisa were dead, and Penny was off with Hope on the road.

It had rained and frozen the night before, so the trees along the river bottom glittered with ice, and it hurt the eyes to look where the sun touched the hill behind the Burkeholder farm. All the gate latches were ice crusted and Lewis Burkeholder had to break each latch open when he went out to feed. He unrolled a big round bale for the cows and stuffed another in the calf creep. The ewes weren't due to lamb until spring, so Lewis was feeding them square baled alfalfa. Nop invariably accompanied Lewis on his rounds, and they'd been working together for so many years, sometimes two or three days would go by without Lewis giving Nop a command. Nop would have liked Lewis to talk more but Lewis had fallen silent.

When the pair came back to the farmhouse, Preacher Shumway's red Fiesta was parked in the dooryard. "Nop why don't you stay outside for awhile," Lewis said, and shook the hay chaff from his pant cuffs before he went inside.

Nop was glad enough to make his morning inspection of the barnyard, glad to initial the Preacher's tire. As he got older, routine became more important. Nop never wondered about Hope, though sometimes he dreamed of the younger dog. Sometimes he dreamed about his mate for so many years, Bit O' Scot, run over by the mail truck, or the Stink Dog, who'd simply failed to rise from her bed one morning. Sometimes he dreamed about people, but usually he dreamed about sheep or other dogs. Now he sniffed where a polecat had visited two nights ago, digging his conical depression after grubs. Nop made certain the polecat wasn't going to return by marking that spot too.

Inside the house, his untouched cup of tea steaming at his elbow, the Preacher was saying, "May God grant these good folks some understanding of what has happened. Through Jesus Christ our Lord . . ."

"And please watch over Penny," Beverly Burkeholder said, her eyes squeezed tight shut.

Lewis waited in the doorway while his wife and the Preacher prayed, and now he set his crook and hat on their hooks, peeled off his heavy woolen jacket and said, "Mighty pretty out there, the ice on the trees and all."

"Good mornin', Lewis," the Preacher said. "I just thought I'd stop by and see how you folks were doin'."

"Oh really, we're fine," Beverly said too brightly.

"Could be better," Lewis said. "We still haven't heard a word from Penny. I got a copy of the *Ranch Dog Trainer* Wednesday and she came third at the sheepdog trial in Fort Worth, Texas. I didn't know most of the handlers she was running against."

"Have you thought about, uh, calling the folks you do know? Maybe they can put you in touch."

Beverly had lost weight and could fit into clothes she hadn't been able to wear in years. Her face was drawn and lined and her black hair was streaked with gray.

Lewis went to the coffee pot. "Penny knows we love her," he said. "When she's ready, she'll give us a call."

IN THE SEPTEMBER TWENTY-EIGHTH *Clarke County Gazette,* the headline said: ACCIDENT CLAIMS THE LIFE OF WHITE POST FARMER AND DAUGHTER

Had that been the whole of it, blunt and plain, the Burkeholders might have healed quicker. It is small things they cannot forget: Lisa's outfit (red skirt, brown overblouse, white socks, tennis shoes) she'd worn that morning when she passed her grandparents' farmhouse. The way she lifted her hand when Beverly waved from the window. And Lisa turned away, resolutely, and Beverly dreams Lisa was turning her face toward her death, rushing toward it.

And Mark's truck: the tie-rod ends were loose, so Lewis had taken the truck down to Crossroads Exxon to have it fixed, and though Lewis knows perfectly well the job was done carefully, that there was nothing wrong with Mark's truck, Lewis dreams of coming around the outside of the curve in the rain and the semi appearing through the rain curtain and Mark jerking the wheel and trying to stay on the road after the semi sideswiped him and not having enough steering to do the job.

Lewis *knows* the steering wasn't bad, but he cannot *believe* it, and he tiptoes downstairs, not to wake his wife, who lies awake anyway while he sits by the dying living room fire and worries about the steering of that truck and, nowadays, when he has mechanical work on his truck or tractor he never takes it to Crossroads Exxon.

Lewis, a stubborn man impatient with concepts, dreamed about tie-rod ends. Beverly, who was a better Christian, dreamed about Lisa going to her own death, with determination. When she told Preacher Shumway, she asked, "Was she going to meet Jesus?"

The preacher, a kind man, said, "Perhaps she was. Lisa is with Jesus now."

But how could she have known?"

The Preacher was one man tending to the spiritual needs of a congregation of 160 souls. Monday night was Bible study, Tuesday night, congregational care, Wednesday was his own, Thursday was the evangelism committee and choir, Friday was the foodbank. Saturday he traveled to Strasburg for the meetings of the Presbytery. He'd known Beverly Burkeholder fairly well before the accident and seen her weekly since.

"We heard from that trucker's insurance company," Beverly said. "They say it was Mark's fault, that he was 'driving too fast for conditions.' How can they tell a lie like that? That semi truck forced Mark off the road into that pond . . ." (Beverly had a memory flash of what the rescue squad man had told them. No doubt the man had meant a kindness, to tell mother and daughter how brave Mark had been at the end. "That pond is right deep," he'd said. "Wasn't any of that pickup showing from the road. When we towed her out, the driver—that was your husband, ma'am—he had his arms around the child. Until the last he held her up to breathe that last pocket of air."

That became Penny's detail. She couldn't think of the accident without picturing her daughter, Lisa, in the pickup cab, doors jammed, under twenty feet of water, held up to the last pocket of air as her father's drowning hands weakened. Penny's detail was her daughter's final terror.

Beverly, who'd been a practical farm woman all her life, shied at that picture, refused it, believed the child was dead as soon as the truck submerged, that like any other animal Lisa'd been too busy dying to feel much one way or the other.

Since she was a child, Penny had been skeptical about life, readier to understand reverses than pleasures and now life played into her hand. Somewhere deep in her soul, Penny had expected something like this: hadn't she been too happy?

Two years ago, Mark attended sheep shearing school down at Steeles Tavern, and after shearing the Burkeholder flock, he went on the road, spring and fall, sometimes with another shearer, sometimes alone. On a good day, shearing a big flock, Mark could pocket two hundred and fifty dollars, and since he'd sleep with the farm family and eat their meals, most of that was profit. From February until June he sheared six, seven days a week. June, July, August, he'd stay on the farm for the haymaking. In September, they planted rye and next year's alfalfa. Penny'd always been a good hand with livestock and was in charge of animal rations and medical care. Penny started selling freezer lambs to Washington customers. With I–64 finished, the DC suburbs were only an hour away, and during Apple Blossom Festival in Winchester, Lewis and Penny would put on sheepdog demonstrations and pass out leaflets about their "naturally reared lambs—no antibiotics, no hormones" and take orders.

Penny substituted at Lisa's school, and though sometimes

it was awkward to be called in at the last minute to teach, any grade from one through nine, the money came in handy: she'd earmarked every penny for Lisa's education, and the account already held more than a thousand dollars.

Like most married couples, Mark and Penny drew close for periods of time then moved further apart. There was a rhythm to this motion, like the beating of a heart. They'd get too dear to each other and Mark'd just naturally have to go off hunting, or go down the road to help Junior Maxwell restore his 1953 Dodge Power Wagon. Junior had the body off it and the frame sandblasted and primed.

When Mark was off shearing, Penny took her meals at the big house with Lewis and Beverly.

Beverly's father, Carl Obenschain, had died three years ago, and though they'd seen it coming—Carl had survived two strokes—he was a bigger loss when he was gone than he'd been a presence when he was alive. Mrs. Obenschain was in the Mennonite home.

Lewis Burkeholder wasn't a real regular churchgoer, just Christmas and Thanksgiving and Easter, but after their granddaughter died, he accompanied Beverly most of the time. In church Beverly prayed and Lewis looked at the preacher and listened, as if any minute something would explain his loss.

That expectant look on Lewis's face distressed the preacher, and some parishioners remarked that Preacher Shumway's sermons certainly were "interesting" these days. On some Sundays, the young preacher outspoke himself, spoke as if inspired by the Holy Spirit, oblivious of his congregation, his wife sitting in the front row of the choir, and when he'd finished, wrung dry, there'd be Lewis Burkeholder's sturdy face, expectant, unsatisfied.

The day after the accident, Lewis made the arrangements for the funeral, picked out the coffins too. Penny had looked him in the eye, his own daughter, and said, "What difference does it make what they're buried in," which shocked Lewis so much he never told Beverly.

Lewis knew George Hansen from the White Post VFD. George wasn't much for answering fire calls in the middle of the night but he'd show up to cook for every chicken barbecue. George's father, Old Bob Hansen, had buried Lewis's parents, and now the son was to bury Lewis's son-in-law and granddaughter. Lisa'd upset the steady progress country people expected from the boisterous cradle to the dignity of the grave.

Beverly's sister and her husband came for Family Night, and a couple of Lewis's cousins drove over from Martinsville. Mark's mother came all the way from Ohio. George Hansen opened his biggest parlor for the occasion, the one they'd redone with the peach paint and recessed lighting just that summer, George and his wife, Emily, doing the painting themselves. Under the flower perfumes, you could smell the faint bitterness of fresh paint.

Lewis and Beverly sat in the viewing room at the foot of the smaller coffin. Other kin waited in the parlor, just outside. "Yes it is sad, and her so young." Penny kept about as far from the coffins as she could get.

And as the women (and men) came to her and took her hand or gave her a hug and said, I'm so sorry, or How could this have happened? she said, "Thank you. Thank you for coming."

George Hansen greeted everybody at the door, in the hallway where they could hang up their coats and take off their galoshes. George made sure everybody signed the little book he'd give to the family later, along with the record of who'd sent flowers.

The White Post VFD had voted to send a forty-five-dollar funeral wreath. Beverly's sister had sent another large display, dahlias, which balanced the VFD on the right-hand side. The most expensive tribute came from Lisa's classmates. The whole school had contributed and a great spray of chrysanthemums loomed above the coffins with a ribbon that said TODAY, THOU ART WITH ME IN PARADISE.

State Assemblyman John Purdy touched Lewis's elbow. "Lewis, a tragedy," and shook Lewis's hand and headed for the thickest crowd to talk hunting and fishing, maybe politic a little. Billy Harkenrude, the school principal, made an appearance, three of the county's four supervisors.

Lisa's teacher, Mrs. Lynch, arrived in her best blue Sunday dress and her seed pearls, and her husband came in behind, like a dinghy towed by a cruise ship.

"Lisa was a wonderful child," she said. She took Penny's hand in her own and patted the back of Penny's rougher one. "We'll all miss her so much."

"Thank you. Thank you for coming."

"Dear, what will you do?"

Penny's eyes focused, recognized the teacher talking to her. She said, "I don't know."

Little Melissa Dowd, same age as Lisa, brunette where Lisa had black hair, didn't take off her blue coat, wouldn't, and it stood out from her short body like she was a Christmas tree ornament. With one hand she was attached to her father, a round man with three chins who was the butcher at the slaughterhouse in Stephen's city and whose normally merry face was solemn and bug-eyed for this occasion. Like Humpty-Dumpty and Alice the pair marched toward the back room that held all the death. Melissa's hand-me-down coat's sleeves were too long. As the child neared the room where her best friend lay, she took a fresh grip of her daddy's hand. They were silhouetted by the lights over the coffins. "I wish Lisa wasn't dead," Melissa said firmly.

And it was Beverly—who loved children, talked easily to children—whose eyes gushed tears so she had to turn away as Lewis said in a deep gravely voice, "Yes, honey. That's what we wish too."

Penny bolted and pushed by George Hansen. "Stuffy," she said, though it wasn't, though George kept everything at a pleasant sixty-five degrees. Outside on the concrete stoop she looked at all the cars and pickup trucks, waiting like so many metal insects to ferry their people home.

The door opened behind her and Lewis Burkeholder took his daughter's arm. "Right brisk out here," he said. He took his old pipe out of his pocket and fumbled around for tobacco but didn't find any, since he'd stopped smoking his pipe (at Beverly's urging) two years ago. He stuck his pipe in his mouth anyway.

"Silly damn thing," he said. "I suppose I should throw it away. You remember that blue teething ring, with the silver handle Aunt Helen sent to Lisa?

He stopped talking and pocketed his pipe and blew his nose.

Melissa and her dad came out and Mr. Dowd shook Lewis's hand and shook his head sorrowfully and said, "ma'am," and led his daughter to his car.

After their headlights came on, Penny said, "If he doesn't lose some weight he's going to leave that child an orphan."

Lewis said, "I don't know what a child thinks. I don't know

when we should protect them. Out here in the country they see dead creatures all the time." He blew his nose again and said, "Twenty years ago you'd look up at the Blue Ridge and not see a single light; all those houses up there now. That child came to say good-bye."

"Daddy," Penny said, "I know I'm embarrassing you, hanging back like this, shunning your friends. I don't have any thing to say."

"Uh-huh. I don't know there is anything to say. It's just words, that's all: words.

Lewis went back inside to sit beside his wife of thirty years beside the coffins of their son-in-law and their grand-daughter.

The evening of the accident, women had started arriving at the Burkeholder house, bearing casseroles to feed the family and their guests, dozens of plastic containers labeled with their owners' names. They arrived swiftly, and those casseroles of tuna, and macaroni and cheese, and lasagna, and sloppy joe mix, and fish loaf became death too, as inevitable as sorrow.

The mourners dropped by until eleven o'clock, awkward, the men standing on the front porch, caps in hand. "He was a good man, Lewis. And that poor little girl . . ." "I had a boy killed on the tractor myself, wasn't much older'n Mark and I know how you must feel."

Caught up in the duties of greeting mourners, taking their coats, getting them coffee and cake, Lewis didn't really feel like anything but a host, ushering those who'd come to comfort him. One of the Puffenbarger women manned the phone. "Burkeholder residence . . . Hello, Audrey. Yes, Beverly's here." Or "No, I'm sorry, Penny can't take the phone right now, would you like to talk to Lewis?"

After the last mourner left, Lewis took the phone off the hook and, for the first time since three years ago when they'd all gone to Virginia Beach on vacation, he bolted the front door. "Penny," he said, "you might as well stay with us tonight."

Without a word, Penny went upstairs to her old bedroom at the head of the stairs.

Neighbor men had done the chores, fed the stock, even put out food for Nop and Hope, the young dog Lewis was training.

"Beverly," Lewis said. "You must be exhausted."

She said, "Lewis, this is the worst day of my life."

"Yes. Come to bed."

Beverly didn't sleep a wink all night, tossing and turning so bad she was up stoking the fires before dawn. Lewis slept like he was dead himself until ten o'clock, when he woke with a jerk, looked at the high white ceiling of what had been his parents' bedroom and grandparents' before, and wondered where he was, who he was, what day it was. It all came flooding back to him and his heart broke.

That day, nobody walked the dogs or did any work with them, and Hope and Nop stayed beside the barn, where they could watch all the comings and goings. Usually Nop barked when strange cars arrived at the farm, he didn't care for strangers, but he held his tongue today.

Hope was worried. Whatever threatens the human household threatens the dog's world tenfold.

All these people dressed in their Sunday best.

"It is death," Nop said, because there is no mistaking death's presence, and he knew that the trailer where Penny and Mark and Lisa lived was cold and empty.

At noon, when nobody came to exercise them, the two dogs walked a half mile down to the river. The willows beside the river glistened with ice and the shoreline was rimed with ice and very far overhead a small flight of Canada geese headed south, its leader chanting *er-whonk, er-whonk.*

Hope wanted to sniff after some deer that had visited the river, but Nop was looking back nervously at the house, half expecting Lewis's whistle. He'd been stolen as a young dog, and ever after Nop had been uneasy away from Lewis. Nop set off resolutely home and the younger dog ran along beside, licking at his mouth, asking silly questions.

Beverly and Lewis watched them from the screened-in back porch. She said, "It's like nothing means anything." She gestured at the farm, the fields they'd cultivated and preserved, the garden space that had fed her family and Lord knows how many families before them, the barn full of hay, the blue Harvestore topped with chopped corn for the winter to come, the woodshed crammed with dry oak, the racks of wood stacked against its end walls, even the dogs—Beverly's gesture dismissed them all.

Lewis's mouth was dry. "Yeah," he said. "We should go back inside."

Saturday morning, the graveside was bitter, with the wind skimming flecks of ice off the ground and the Preacher bundled up to the neck, wearing his black scarf, and topcoat, everybody hatless and their ears turning red. Preacher Shumway read the internment service for a husband and his daughter, the daughter he'd tried in vain to save. "Greater love hath no man," he said.

Penny stood with the family under the awning, before the two coffins, side by side, the mound of earth covered with

AstroTurf. George Hansen kept the limousine running so it'd be warm for the mourners on the way home.

Lisa and Mark Hilyer were buried in the old part of the White Post cemetary beside Burkeholders they'd never met, with space left for Penny and Lewis and Beverly when their time came.

Penny was first away from the gravesite, first into the limousine, huddled in the far back, small as she could get.

Beverly was stunned. Four days to wrap up lives that had taken years to nurture, and nothing left but dry eyes and grainy eyelids and the feeling that perhaps she ought to take a shower.

Penny went to her trailer and for three days there was no sign of her, no tracks coming in or out, except the smoke from her chimney. The insurance man called Lewis when he couldn't get through to Penny because she'd left the phone off the hook.

"Look, Lewis," he said, "we can pay off on Mark's truck right away, but the driver of that semi, he was insured out in New Mexico, and they won't pay any settlement until there's a finding he was to blame. Yes, everybody knows that semi forced Mark off the road, but their lawyer. . . . Don't worry, Lewis, I'll see Penny gets taken care of, it's just gonna take time. You know how these things are."

The insurance on Mark's truck paid $600. Lewis took the check down to the trailer.

"Daddy," Penny said, "Mark wouldn't have taken a thousand dollars for that truck. I didn't want a new truck, I want Mark's truck fixed."

Lewis shook his head. "Honey, you don't want that old truck anymore, not now the water's got into it."

"Where'd it go? Where'd they take it? How do I know there wasn't something in it I wanted?"

61

"Honey, the rescue squad went through the truck at the scene, emptied the glove compartment and behind the seat. I know six hundred isn't much . . ."

"I want a truck just like I had. There's all that money I put away for Lisa's college: a thousand two hundred forty-five dollars."

Back in his own kitchen, Lewis looked out at the falling snow and said, "Beverly, I don't know how she can live in that mess. Clothes dropped wherever she took 'em off, sink full of dirty dishes."

Beverly touched her husband's cheek. "Hush, Lewis. It's just something she's got to go through."

But the next morning, Lewis was back on his daughter's doorstep, with Hope. The dog was muscular, stocky and calm. His eyes said he found the world good, and interesting, and "Howdy, stranger!"

Although it was well past sunup, Penny came to the door in her bathrobe. Behind her the TV was playing one of those morning shows, the host murmuring sympathetically to some movie star, how hard it was, celebrity, how hard.

"G'morning," Lewis said. "I brought you this Hope dog."

Penny was puzzled. "That's the dog you're going to trial . . ."

"Not anymore I'm not. Him and me, we had a falling out. He needs somebody else. You used to be fair shakes as a trainer. Here." He passed her the dog's lead.

The dog looked up, puzzled. Some human ritual going on here, involving him, he wasn't quite sure how. His eyebrows furrowed.

"What am I supposed to do with a dog?"

Lewis looked away over the fields. "Those maiden ewes are in the river pasture. You can work with them, you want to."

"I can't even take care of myself. How can I take care of a dog?"

Lewis shrugged. "Train him up and sell him. Put a couple months into him, you can get a thousand, twelve hundred, give me four hundred for my share."

"Daddy, please." She held the dog's leash as slack as she could.

"Supposed to be sunny tomorrow," Lewis said. Crows flew over, cawing their way to the riverbank. "You know how it is—once you've fallen out with a dog there's no use working with him. This fella might make a dog in the right hands." And he jammed his hands deep into his pocket and walked away and the dog looked at Lewis, looked at the woman, wagged his tail once, stood still.

"Oh you might as well come in. There's been no dog here since Stink died." She unfastened his leash and got a glass of Diet Pepsi from a liter on the countertop and sat down in the recliner right in front of the TV.

The dog waited, seeking a cue, and when he didn't get one, investigated his new habitat, room by room, yard by yard. What he smelled was the fading odors of two other people and this woman, a small leak where the gas line attached to the stove, the bitter stink of freon behind the refrigerator, the residual smell of the dog who'd been here years ago, who'd slept right behind the woodbox, marking the wall with her wet tail. He smelled the remnants of meals Penny had made for herself, some scorched. In the living room, he sniffed at a heap of woman's clothes, pawed at them, much as his ancestors arranged the leaves and twigs of their night's bedding, and flumped down.

"Hey, who told you you could use my blue jeans for a bed?"

Hope smiled in his most charming manner—and he was a dog of considerable charm.

"Come on now, get off those."

Hope yawned hugely and moved to the corner where Penny's funeral dress and slip lay where she'd dropped them.

"Now don't you lie on that. You know what it cost to take that to the cleaners?"

Hope wagged at her, puzzled. If he wasn't supposed to lie on that stuff, why was it on the floor?

"Alright, alright," she said and shed her robe and went to the dresser for clean underthings and put on the very jeans Hope'd been lying on ("How nice," he thought, "she likes me"), and scooped up the dirty clothes, and carried them to the washer. Hope stood in the doorway, baffled.

"Why are you in my way all the time?" she said, as she bustled back and forth. "Here, come over here." She pointed at the space behind the woodbox where the other dog had lain so long ago, and Hope went there and looked at her. "Lie down," she said, and Hope did.

While the washer was running, Penny hung up her funeral dress and the bathrobe too. With the noise from the washing machine she couldn't hear the TV so she turned it off; it shrank into a dot on the screen.

Penny pushed dirty dishes aside and opened a can of Chunky Beef soup and heated it until it boiled, and ate it out of the pot with a spoon. Afterward, she took the can to the garbage pail. A milk jug fell out, and when she tried to cram everything there wasn't any more room, so she lugged the can out beside the yard. Mark used to take the trash to the dump. All my life, she thought, I've had some man to take care of me, first Daddy then Mark and now Daddy again.

Penny expected the dog to take off for the main house, to run back to Lewis, but he busied himself inspecting his new turf and, apparently satisfied, he rolled on his back, flipped over, and scooped up snow with his nose and lifted his head, a scruff of snow still on his nose, to see if she'd got the joke.

"That's all I need," she said, "another fool dog."

That evening Penny came to the big house to borrow dog food, and when Lewis asked her was Hope settling in, she said, "That dog is a real piece of work." Lewis asked Penny if she wanted to look through her mail, they'd been saving it. No, she didn't. Would Beverly sort through and take out the bills, she didn't want to read any of the letters.

That was Thursday. Saturday, Lewis and Penny went into Winchester to see if they could find a truck.

Penny was doing okay, even ate a small salad at Wendy's. Lewis told her there was a vacancy—full time—at the elementary school. Billy Hess, the principal, had called. "I don't want it," she said.

Lewis said, "But, honey, you got to do something."

She looked him right in the eye. "Why's that?"

He said, "If we don't have any luck with the car dealers, maybe we can find something in the newspaper."

That evening, Penny took Hope out for training. The ewes were in a five-acre meadow beside the river. Hope sailed toward them, for no conscious reason except what his genetics

65

told his muscles to do—he wouldn't have heeded a command from Penny had she commanded him. He came around behind the sheep, and, when his genes said "stop," he stopped.

The sheep moved toward Penny, and Hope harried them, shifting from one side to the other until his brain clicked in: *"Where is my master?"* and he peered over the sheep to locate Penny, who'd moved, so Hope changed directions to keep the sheep coming straight to her.

A sheepdog's most basic instinct is to fetch sheep to his master, and it was this instinct Penny used. She walked backward, dodged from side to side, so the dog would learn where he had to be. Penny never uttered a command; she showed the dog what made sense. They kept at it for an hour as the winter light faded and went blue, before Penny called Hope off. "That'll do, here," and he was tired enough to quit and, truth be told, he was proud of himself too.

In the trailer, Penny stoked the stove, set down a bowl of fresh water for Hope, washed one load of dishes, dried and put them away, washed a second load and left those in the rack.

"That puts a dent in it," she muttered. Hope went over to his dinner bowl and paused and looked up at her.

Misreading it, she said, "It's okay. You can eat."

He wagged his tail meaning, that's not the problem.

"Oh," Penny said, "you're one of those." She carried his food into the bathroom and closed the door and moments later heard the crunching as he enjoyed his solitary meal.

The next morning she trained Hope for an hour and cleaned up her trailer. At noon, when her parents came back from church Penny went to the big house to say, "I'm going to give Mark's and Lisa's clothes to the Salvation Army. Would you phone them up?" Beverly did, they'd come Saturday.

Lewis said, "I told Billy you'd be coming to work at the school Thursday morning. If you don't want the job, I should let him know."

Penny said, "Oh, alright."

That night Hope moved from the space behind the stove and slipped into Penny's bedroom and clattered down on the floor, at her bedside. He liked the sound of her breathing and wished to be enfolded in her night smell.

She said, "You sound like a bucket of bones," and he thumped the floor with his tail.

Wednesday morning, they were at it again. Young dogs usually want to get to their sheep, get as close as they can. It's the trainer's task to keep the dog back, to give the dog time and space to think. That magic realm between attack and indifference is where the trainer wants his dog. "Time," Penny commanded. "Hope! Take time."

Wednesday night, Hope got it right, and Thursday morning, before dawn, when the raw wind came clipping down the fields and the sun was just a vague discoloration over the Blue Ridge, Hope got it right three times, and Penny was excited: not happy, just excited.

In the kitchen of the big house, her father looked at his watch but didn't say anything. He didn't invite her to have a cup of breakfast coffee either. "That fellow down at Sunrise Texaco called last night. Said he had a Dodge truck his uncle used to run. It's got high miles but his uncle was old-fashioned, changed the oil every two thousand miles. I've got to get some sheep wormer at the Coop. I'll check over the Dodge if you want me to."

At school Principal Hess told Penny all the kids were getting revved up for Christmas, that some of her students were in the Christmas play, said she'd be paid the same rate as a substitute if she didn't mind.

The kids knew Penny from times she'd substituted before and they'd known Lisa, so Thursday they were quiet, awed by the actual presence of their dead friend's mother. Fourth grade had twenty-four students, more girls than boys. Represented were sons and daughters from sixteen marriages, six separations, and the Smith twins, who were the product of a union unblessed by state or clergy. Half the kids were eligible for the school's free lunch program. Marsha MacKinney, age eight, weighed fifty pounds, stood four feet two, and worried she'd never get any bigger. Ralph Lawson weighed a hundred ten pounds, stood five foot six, and worried he would. Penny had bought groceries at Ewald's Market (Billy Ewald), mineral salts and livestock supplies from Thunder Ridge Farm (Margaret Baxter). Penny stuck to her lesson plan, and when the bell rang at 3:05 she reminded them of their homework and they said yes ma'am or nodded their heads.

Principal Hess stuck his head in the door as Penny was putting on her coat. "How'd it go? Anything I can do? Anything at all."

Lewis was parked behind the school buses, his exhaust pluming white smoke in the frosty air. He said the Dodge truck was worth a looksee. It had a camper with stickers on it: HUNTING: THE AMERICAN WAY and WHEN THE TAILGATE DROPS THE BS STOPS. The camper latch was busted and the owner said his uncle had lost the key when he was out fishing and had to break the lock to get in.

"I got to have fourteen hundred for it," he said. Penny wrote him a check for twelve fifty.

When they got back to the farm, Lewis wanted her to wait

in the truck while he brought Beverly out to see. "Dad," she said, "it's just an old pickup truck. Besides, Hope's been locked up all day."

After dinner (Lean Cuisine: Fettucini Alfredo) Penny went into the front room to watch TV and once she'd settled on the couch, Hope cocked an eye, put one paw on the armchair, another, unlawfully flumped himself into the seat and grinned at her. She smiled at his joke. "Okay, I get it," she said. "Now get down off there."

On Saturday the Salvation Army came for Lisa's and Mark's things, a pair of elderly black men from Winchester who removed their caps each time they came into the trailer. "Yes, ma'am," they said and "No, ma'am," and "Are you sure you want all these things to go?" And one said, "I have a niece who'd like to have this," holding up Lisa's Sunday jumper.

Beverly came to help but kept bursting into tears, so Penny asked her to stay in the kitchen, make some coffee or something.

Sunday, Penny and the dog walked nearly twenty miles. Farms were side by side along the river bottom and Penny knew all the farmers, so she ignored the no trespassing, no hunting signs, and when one farmer came on his tractor to investigate, he gave her a wave.

That night Penny was ravenous and ate two TV dinners. She showered so she wouldn't need to in the morning. She sat on the edge of the bed she'd shared with her husband. "At least that junk is out of here," she said.

Hope lifted his head and sniffed. "I will guard thee against ghosts," he said.

She said, "Lie down and stop padding around."

Monday, Tuesday, at school; okay. By Wednesday, the novelty of a bereaved mother as teacher had worn off. The first sign of the return of the old order was when Ralph Lawson stole Margaret Baxter's arithmetic book and passed the book around the class.

Little Margaret was nonplussed. "Okay, you guys," she said, "who's got it? I want my book back right now." Repeating a line she'd heard from her parents, she said, "Do you think I'm made of money?"

"I'll tell you what you're made of," Ralph whispered, and proceeded to do just that.

Penny said, "Alright Ralph, that's enough. That'll do."

Saturday morning, Penny telephoned. "Come down, Daddy," she said. "I've got something to show you."

Out in the training field, the young dog behaved impeccably, balancing his sheep as accurately as a plumb bob, keeping a distance, stopping on command, standing until Penny called him on.

"Well?" Penny demanded.

"He's a real crackerjack," her father said slowly. "Reminds me of the first time I ever ran his father at a trial . . ."

"But?"

Lewis stuck his hands deep in his pockets. "Might be you're bringing him on too quick," he said.

Penny bristled. "Until he's got flanks, he can't start to drive."

"You've got plenty time for that," Lewis said.

"He'll need to drive in the open."

"Honey, he's just fourteen months. He's too young for open trials."

"Eikamp's Rex was two when he won the Nationals."

70

"That was Eikamp's Rex."

Later, when Lewis looked out the window, Penny was down in the field, training.

That's what she did, mornings and evenings, train her dog. On weekends, after Hope's morning bout she'd walk him twenty-five miles a day over snow, and with all his dashing around, Hope was doing four times that.

Hope was happy. He'd found a world perfectly designed for him—as much work as he could do until his attention wavered, and then off for a run until he tired. Hope got hard, stretched muscles over his bones. Once, rushing to get through a farm gate before Penny closed it, Hope smacked into Penny's legs and Penny fell, and when her senses returned, here was this dog circling her whining, worried to death. She limped into school Monday morning, and when Margaret Baxter asked what had happened she said she'd fallen on the ice. Each time Penny locked up Hope it was like she was leaving her life behind.

While the kids read their lessons, Penny's mind wandered. She wondered if she really was pushing Hope too hard. "Yes, Bobby. You can go to the boys' room." She didn't notice the kids' grins—she'd already let two other boys go. Mr. Bahnson, the shop teacher, brought the miscreants back. "You've got more faith in these kids than I do. Wait'll the janitor sees what they did in there." The three boys looked hangdog, and Penny thought that Hope never looked hangdog. When Hope did wrong and she corrected him, sometimes his eyes got hot and red and she thought he wasn't going to defer to her. But, always, he did.

. . .

ON FRIDAY, December twenty-second, three o'clock, Penny came home and disappeared into her trailer. Lewis Burkeholder let the kitchen curtains fall closed. "Penny's home early."

Beverly looked up from her devotional. "Maybe because it's Christmas?"

Lewis yawned. Wood heat made man and dog sleepy, and Old Nop was behind the stove, snoozing. Lewis answered the phone.

"Lewis, it's me, Billy Hess. I don't know how much Penny told you, but it was no big thing."

Through the gap in the curtains Lewis could see Penny and Hope in the training field.

"I'm afraid I don't follow, Billy."

"We all lose our tempers sometime. Penny isn't the first teacher to . . . lose it. She scared him more than hurt him. The Lawson boy was hurting the Baxter girl and Penny stopped it. The Lawson boy's a real terror . . ."

"Listen Billy, I haven't talked to Penny. I'll call you back."

"Just tell her nobody wants her to quit. After Christmas, her job'll be waiting for her."

PENNY WAS OUT in the big field, fifty acres tucked up against the flank of the mountain. A small flock of sheep had gathered on a knoll, perhaps a half mile down the field, and Lewis wouldn't have seen them, except for the orange sun glinting off their wool.

The dog was a dark dot against the snow way out there. The wind kicked up ice flakes from the surface of the snow and whisked them against Lewis's boots, and he wrapped his

72

woolen scarf over his face. Penny stood hipshot, giving no command, showing no impatience.

When the sheep turned to face Hope, Penny put her fingers to her mouth and whistled a single, long blast. Two count, three. Hope was on his feet, marching toward the sheep, implacable.

The sheep angled quietly across the field to Penny's feet and she called Hope, "That'll do, Hope," and Hope came to her, knowing how fine he'd been, delight vibrating off him, and he jumped up then, his snout higher than Penny's head, once, twice, three times.

Lewis stepped into the circle of the woman and her dog. "Cold out here," Lewis noted.

"Oh yeah, I suppose it is." Hope espied an inviting clump of dead broomsedge and snuffled under the golden straw, just like there was something hiding there.

"I got a call from Billy Hess, at the school," Lewis said.

Penny stuck her hands in her pockets. Her eyes were her mother's eyes. For a moment, in the fading winter light, Lewis saw the young woman he'd married forty years ago.

Penny said, "I'm not fit to be around little kids."

Lewis raised his eyebrows and said, "If we don't get into some shelter I'm going to freeze to death."

Hope bounced along, snuffling, thinking that maybe his foolishness could lighten things up a little.

"Hess said it was no big thing, said he wanted you to stay on."

"So I can smack another kid?"

Two Burkeholders, heads bowed, hands in pockets, silhouetted by the dying sun crunched back across the snowy field.

Christmas morning, Lewis gave Beverly some handspun wool he'd picked up in Winchester, and Beverly gave him a sweater. At noon, they went out for the Christmas Buffet at Shoney's. Just the two of them.

Beverly was chipper and burbled like a bobolink and said how nice this was and how nice that was and, Lewis, won't you take a look at this salad bar, but Beverly only took a few things for her plate and didn't eat most of those.

That evening Lewis went out early for the chores and finished well before dark. Although he saw Penny walking with Hope he and Nop walked the other way.

Nop never strayed far from Lewis's side. Nop felt sad, but that might have been the sad light of that time of year. He raised his head to sniff the air: the frozen earth under the snow, the sheep who'd passed this way this morning.

Just yesterday, Nop was sailing over every fence on the place, and now he waited, politely, for Lewis to open the gates. Just yesterday they'd been inseparable on America's trial fields, ranging up and down the country, and victory had become habitual with them. The two old animals trudged back through the winter night to their warm, cheerless home.

LEWIS AND BEVERLY didn't see much of their daughter in the next few weeks. Neighbors, running into Lewis at the feed store or the tractor dealership would say how they'd seen Penny and that young dog "down at the Miller Place" or "halfway to Braxton's Mill."

A little after dinner, on January 12th, which was a Wednesday, Penny knocked and asked if she could come in for a minute, just a minute, I know you're busy, and Beverly put down her knitting and said, "Oh no, dear, we were just going to watch television," and Penny said how she wouldn't want to interrupt their program, and Beverly said it was just MacNeil/Lehrer and they could watch them any night.

"I'm leaving," Penny said. After a moment she added, "There's nothing here for me anymore."

"I'm just making up some herb tea," Beverly said. "Lewis doesn't care for it but I think it's very refreshing. Where are you going, honey?"

"Ma, please don't cry."

Beverly blew her nose into a paper towel, stepped to the counter and scooped three spoonfuls of raspberry tea into her teapot. "I'm sorry," she said. "I don't mean to be so silly."

"Me and Hope are going on the sheepdog trial circuit. There's a trial at the Fort Worth Stock Show and I called 'em up and they'll let us run."

"Open?" Lewis asked.

"That's where the prize money is."

Sweat dropped off Lewis's forehead. Beverly always did like the living room too warm. "If you need us," he said, "just call. Anytime, honey. Anywhere." Lewis felt weak in the knees, but he didn't want Penny to think he was too feeble to help her if she needed it. "That truck runnin' okay?"

She said that it was running just fine. She told her mother if she started to cry again she'd leave right now, and when Beverly did, Penny did.

March 4, 2nd go-round, Tuscon, Arizona
Judge: Bill Berhow, Lavina, Montana

63 open dogs went to the post

1. Ransome Barlow	Bute	95½
2. Roger Schroeder	Don	92
3. Roger Culbreath	Trim	91
4. Bruce Fogt	Molly	90
5. Ted Johnson	Craig	89

MEN TRIAL SHEEPDOGS for the usual metaphysical reasons. Some men seek justice in their own lifetime. Others, a type of immortality. Bill Crowe of Virginia once explained that he trialed, "For the pure intellectual achievement of it." Some men hope that love is proof against adversity. Some trial sheepdogs to forget—bad marriages can make good sheepdog handlers—and others trial to remember: that single moment, the flash of light on a dog's coat, the dog dead now twenty years. A few men trial because that's the only way they can reduce the world to their size; others trial for the raw information trialing provides, a flux they can puzzle over for a lifetime.

When Ransome Barlow's father walked out, Ransome was eleven. His parents never argued, never fought, never threw things at one another, never complained, but one day Ransome's father went off to work and never came home and never sent a note or a postcard. Ransome's mother acted like husbands vanish every day of the week. Ransome's father left a new eighteen-foot skiff with twin Evinrudes, a Yamasaki ATV, a Bultaco dirt bike, a Nikon F-3 camera, and one by one in the months after he left, they were repossessed. Though Ransome's mother was working, she didn't make a single payment on any of them, not one. She didn't make the payments on the Ford Mustang her husband drove away in, either, but never learned if the car was repossessed or not. She worked as the manager of a frozen food wholesaler, she did buy food, did pay the rent, preferred the "Andy Griffith Show" to "Jeopardy," and by the time they found her cancer it had metastasized. She had kept up the payments on her insurance, which was adequate to bury her. Though Ransome was just seventeen, he joined the Marine Corps, and by the time the corps learned he'd lied about his age, he was old enough to stay.

After four years they invited him to reup, promised him a bonus and corporal's stripes, but Ransome said no thanks, he had other plans. Back in Johnson City, he went to the bank for a mortgage on a convenience store on the outskirts of town and worked seven days a week, 7 A.M. to midnight, open Thanksgiving and Christmas, until he owned it outright. Then he hired an elderly couple to take over while he went around the countryside dirt bike racing. He found the dirt bikes simple. Around you went. You ate dust. You got sore. You got deaf. Around you went.

Pure accident brought Ransome to sheepdog trials at the Illinois State Fair. His bike had snapped a camshaft and he went out to the back lot to cool out, and that's where he met his future. His ears were still ringing as the dogs slipped and dodged, he knew they were taking commands but couldn't hear them.

He bought a dog and five sheep and three weeks later, he stepped onto the trial field. He learned:

> Control is a gift.
> The finest control is a delicate grip on chaos.
> Control must be prepared for, trained, invoked.
> Control is self-referential.
> Perfect control retreats before the seeker.

Ransome went through eight dogs, bought one week and re-sold three weeks later, before he found Bute, who'd been imported from Wales as a two-year-old, badly beaten by Jack Crowley in Arizona, and given up on by Jill Kerold in Michigan. Bute was hard and physically powerful, a medium-size dog with deep chest and thick hind legs.

Though Bute came into this country for three thousand, Ransome bought him for five hundred dollars.

Ransome put five ewes in a fifty-foot ring and walked in with Bute, and Bute promptly attacked a ewe, slashing her ham so badly it took twelve stitches.

Next day, another ewe: eight stitches.

Next day, Ransome Barlow got his corrections in just ahead of Bute's teeth and needle and thread stayed in the medicine cabinet.

Fourth day, Bute ignored Ransome's command, dove for a

sheep, and before the dog's jaws could close, Ransome had tackled him and rolled him over in the dirt. Bute's eyes flashed rage and the panicked ewes hurled themselves at the boundary fence and Bute would have savaged Ransome then and there had he not squeezed that black beast's throat until Bute passed out. He knelt there in the dirt beside the dog, wheezing, until Bute opened his eyes.

Bute never again tried to bite a sheep, and Ransome never again laid a hand on him. It wasn't pain or fear of death that bound Bute to Ransome Barlow. Bute had finally found a man as serious as he was.

THE BURKEHOLDERS' PHONE was an old-fashioned wall phone, and since Lewis liked to pace when he talked, its long cord tangled like black spaghetti. It was Ethel Harwood, and country courteous, Lewis discussed the weather: terrible mud in Virginia, impossible to get into the fields. Ethel said it was wet in Texas too. After the weather they talked about dogs. No Lewis didn't have any young dogs. He wasn't trialing much anymore.

Finally Ethel said, "That Hope dog of Penny's is coming on well."

Beverly was in the rocker reading Lenten meditations. "Ethel's seen Penny," Lewis hissed. To Ethel he said, "He's out of Nop, the dam is Florence Wilson's Kate. Penny handling him alright?"

Ethel didn't know why Lewis's daughter had left home and didn't want to make things worse. "Penny's healthy, Lewis. I'd say she's lost too much weight. Her and that dog . . . well, Lewis, you remember how Lewis Pence was with that Star dog, the one he started working before he died. You remember how connected they seemed? That's how it is with Hope and Penny. That dog seems to be reading her mind half the time. She came third. Ransome Barlow and Orin Barnes beat her. Penny's running in Arizona next week. The Saila trial."

Beverly plucked at Lewis's sleeve. "Ask how Penny was dressed. Did she have warm clothes?"

Lewis covered the phone. "Beverly, she's in Texas. You don't need warm clothes in Texas."

"Lewis, please?"

Lewis Burkeholder came from a tradition of keeping family problems inside the family, that's how his parents did, and what he remembered of his grandparents that's how they'd done too. The phone was saying, "Lewis? Lewis, you still there?"

"Yeah. Ethel, look, you're an old friend and well, Beverly is kind of worried, and she wants to know if Penny is dressed warm."

"Lewis Burkeholder, you are an old fool. Put Beverly on the phone."

The women talked for thirty minutes, time for Lewis to look through a country living article in *Farm Journal*. "Oh yes," the farm wife had written. "Farm life can be demanding, but every sunrise is a brand-new day." Usually Lewis would have snorted, but today he examined the picture of the silly woman and her tidy farmhouse and thought that what she'd said was probably true. Lewis closed his eyes and prayed his daughter might be alright.

After Beverly hung up she went into the bathroom and ran water for her face. Penny used to refresh herself in just the same way.

"Oh, Lewis," Beverly said. "I do wish Penny'd come home."

"I think I'll call the insurance company, see if they're making any progress with that trucking outfit. I don't suppose a few dollars would hurt her."

Beverly's face was bright and expectant as a girl's. "Lewis, let's go to Arizona. That Saila trial. You always wanted to go to that trial."

Lewis gaped. "Beverly, I haven't got a dog."

"You can run Nop."

And Nop, hearing his name and knowing something depended on him stretched and yawned and wagged his tail. "I am thy dog and I am willing," he said.

The very next day, Lewis got the motor home started and pulled it to the dooryard gate so Beverly could put the inside in order. He'd wash the exterior as soon as the day warmed enough so his hoses didn't freeze. He walked Nop out into the pasture where Penny had trained.

For the first minutes of his outrun, Nop felt wonderful, like he was a puppy again. But when he came up behind the woolies, his tongue was out a mile. Woolies eyed the dog nervously and one ewe stamped her foot, daring him to come on, but it was just a bluff, and the wise old dog slid toward them.

Though Nop took each of Lewis's flanking commands, Lewis saw how winded he was and called him off.

That afternoon, in forty-degree weather, Lewis put on his oldest coveralls and with a bucket of warm water and ammonia, he cleaned off the exterior of the motor home, scraping bird droppings off the windshield while Beverly's vacuum hummed inside.

Next morning, soon as Lewis finished feeding, he trained

Nop for fifteen minutes and then another long walk. Later, he drove into Strasburg and talked to a young fellow who'd worked for him before, asked him to come out and feed the cows and sheep "and put out a little kibble for the barn cats."

That evening, Lewis and Nop walked so long they came home by starlight. Beverly said, "I believe you're losing a little weight Lewis."

He said, "Pass me more of that stew."

Beverly had to go into Winchester to get her hair done and ask someone to take her Sunday school class. She asked Preacher Shumway to look in on her mother.

"Of course," the preacher said. "But Beverly, will Penny . . . ?"

Beverly said, "Don't you tell me it isn't going to work. I don't have a single expectation. Lewis and me are just going out west to a sheepdog trial, that's all. That's why we bought that motor home in the first place."

"I'll pray for you. All of you."

And Beverly answered, with some of her old asperity, that if he wanted to pray, wasn't anybody going to stop him, but the Burkeholders had got on alright in the world so far without his prayers and she didn't reckon they'd need any now.

That night, over supper, she told Lewis what she had said and giggled about it. "Of course, I'll have to call and apologize."

Nop was on his blanket behind the stove. The fire crackled in the wood stove. That night, for the first time since their granddaughter died, Lewis and Beverly Burkeholder were together as man and wife. As always, each wondered afterward why they'd been apart so long.

. . .

THURSDAY MORNING, well before sunrise, Lewis Burkeholder toted Beverly's brown paper bags from the house to the motor home's kitchenette. "Beverly," he said, "there'll probably be some supermarkets in Arizona. I think they got supermarkets in the west now."

Nop traveled underneath Beverly's feet with his snout on the transmission hump. The road rumbled by under his body and gears whirled in their fluids and tractor trailers boomed past and sometimes Lewis would turn on the radio to check the weather. Younger, Nop had traveled thousands of miles to sheepdog trials and he rather enjoyed traveling, meeting new scents, new dogs, new sheep, and he enjoyed the trial too, the risk and adventure.

The motor home buzzed down I-81 at fifty-five miles per hour. It handled like Lewis's heavy farm truck only the steering and brakes were better.

"We'll pick up US40 outside of Knoxville and I figure we'll find a place to stop somewhere between Nashville and Memphis."

Beverly said, "I hope Penny won't be upset to see us."

"Well, if she is, she is. I've got as much right as anybody to enter a sheepdog trial."

"Don't get huffy, dear."

At noon, Beverly went in back to make sandwiches. "Would you like toast?"

Lewis' mildly nervous about the prospect of someone cooking toast while traveling fifty-five miles an hour down the interstate, said, no thanks, untoasted was fine.

They pulled into an RV camp at dusk and as soon as Lewis hooked up the power and the plumbing, he put Nop on a leash and strolled down to the muddy creek that bordered the place. "Now don't you go drinkin' out of that," Lewis said. "We've got home water in the motor home."

That second morning, they set out before dawn, didn't stop except for gas and fifteen minutes at noon to let Nop stretch his legs, and found a campground west of Amarillo, Texas. Beverly stretched while Nop sniffed the ornamental bushes planted between the parking spots. The sky was enormous over the plains and a thin line of sunset lay orange along the horizon. "My," Beverly said. "Oh my."

Nop was used to more exercise, and that night he prowled his sleeping shelf until Lewis told him to cut it out. Nop lay awake late, listening to the howl of the coyotes, so far away and faint no human could have known what they were. Nop knew.

Big dog trials are all the same. Motor homes and campers in a line behind the course and the awnings are out and kids are running through the guy wires and the dogs are chained underneath or in crates out back, and in the dusk a few people are walking their dogs, as they sniff their sniffs, trump the previous dog's ace.

No big trial is the same. Though the rules are standardized and judges, for the most part, consistent, sheep vary tremendously. In Arizona they were wild range merinos, and if a man came near them, they'd trample one another in a panic to flee.

And each course is different. Some face a steep hill, some are flat, some like sagebrushy Saila, are rumpled and irregular, so the man can always see the sheep, but the dog cannot. This evening, a few handlers were out on the sagebrush plains stooping to dog height, trying to guess what their dogs will see and sense tomorrow under the Arizona sun.

"Look, Lewis. There's Penny's truck."

"She's been on some muddy roads. I don't see Penny."

Parked between an Ohio camper and a motor home with Mississippi plates, Lewis leveled his vehicle while Nop wandered around renewing old acquaintances. There were dogs here Nop had run against when they were just "started"—two-year-old youngsters—with no more idea of a trial course than the dog in the moon. Now gray-snouted dogs looked up as Nop walked by and thumped their tails.

"Lewis, hello. Damn it's good to see you. Is that Beverly in there?"

"Uh-huh. Couldn't keep her away. How are you, Miz Harwood?" Lewis touched the brim of his Texas hat.

"Oh, Lewis, don't be such a stick-in-the-mud." And Ethel Harwood gave him a good squeeze. She touched Nop's head. "And how are you, Mr. Nop? I swear he hasn't aged a bit."

"He's slowed down some, but so have I. Have you seen Penny?"

"She was here earlier but she and some others went out to work dogs. She and that Hope dog make a good team, but they didn't have much luck out the first go-round. Does she know you're here?"

Lewis blew between his lips. "Don't reckon she does."

The trial's host said he was real pleased Lewis could get out here this year and urged Beverly to get into the chow line for some "real Arizona chili." " 'Course there's burgers if you'd prefer," he added.

Lewis talked dogs, gravely accepted a few belated condolences. "I meant to write, Lewis, but I never got around to it."

The host asked Lewis, was the food okay. And Lewis said sure, sure it was. Driving all day had ruined his appetite.

Handlers and dogs packed the back of Ransome Barlow's pickup. Penny sat on the far side of the cab, pale faced in the dashlights. When Hope jumped out he lifted his snout and beelined right to where Lewis and Beverly were standing.

"Hullo Hope, Hey Penny! Over here, Penny!"

Penny came directly to her mother and father and asked, "What are you doing here?"

Lewis swallowed the first thing he thought to say; second thing too. As he got older, he had got a firmer grip on his temper. "Well," he said slowly, "Beverly and I thought we'd come out and I'd run Nop, see how much he's still got in him. We haven't been off the farm—"

"I didn't mean that," Penny said. "I was just so surprised to see you. Wait'll you see Hope run. He's tremendous. I had him out tonight on Navaho sheep and they got up in the rocks and those rank sheep ran another dog off but they took one look at Hope and filed out as meek as lambs."

Beverly's face was wet when she embraced her daughter. "Honey, honey. Old place sure hasn't been the same without you."

Penny inspected the motor home, like she really cared, like she actually did think her mother's cheerful curtains were "terrific," like she'd never been inside the motor home before in her life. She said, "This is exactly like a sailboat," and then, "Of course I've never been inside a sailboat but I'll bet this is how they are." Beverly poured ice tea, but Penny wouldn't sit, said, "No, no," she could only stay a minute, and told about lambing sheep in Texas. And when that subject was exhausted, she made a lateral move into the subject of mohair goats, how they had to be housed after they were shorn or they'd catch pneumonia.

Beverly said, "But, honey, how have you been? Are you doin' okay? Are you in good spirits?"

"Yeah, Mom, fine." And Penny kissed her mother on the cheek and said she had to go, and Lewis thought to ask her where, in the night, she had to go but again held his tongue. Instead he said, "We'll have plenty of time to talk tomorrow."

Once she'd gone, silence rushed into that motor home like a flood tide. On his shelf, Nop raised his head, and maybe he was just responding to some distant coyote when he got a hot look in his eyes, and howled.

"Hush up now," Lewis said. "Don't you get started."

Nop was abashed and scuffed his bedding, pretending some other dog, not he, had raised the hackles of every other dog in the handlers' encampment. One or two other dogs had taken up Nop's howl, and shouts—"Roy, Hush," "Kep, you quit that racket"—echoed until it fell quiet again.

As the Burkeholders readied for bed, the moon came up, gleaming on silver dog trailers and silent motor homes. Lewis lay next to his wife as western moonlight flooded through the window over the tiny kitchen table.

"So this is Arizona," Beverly said.

THE NEXT MORNING, the first dogs ran as soon as there was light to see. Lewis was scheduled to run at noon, Penny in the late afternoon. After breakfast, Lewis went outside with a cup of coffee. It was cool yet and the merinos were flying whenever a dog put too much pressure on them.

Ethel Harwood found Penny beside Ransome Barlow, critiquing each run.

"I'd hit him a couple points for that," Barlow was saying as a young dog swerved too tight at the post.

"Excuse me, Penny. Could I have a word with you?"

"It'll have to wait Miz Harwood. After this run I promised to go out back and put out sheep."

"Tonight," Ethel said, "we're all having dinner in town."

And she didn't budge, kept the pressure on until Penny said, "Sure. I just hope we have something to celebrate." Penny added, "Hope. Or Nop."

Left to their own devices, sheep graze in the cool of the early morning and when it heats up, around ten o'clock, they bed down in the shade. These trial sheep had been penned all morning with no chance to graze and now it was hot and they were pushed onto the course, hungry and cranky.

One of Nop's sheep had lost an eye to pinkeye as a lamb, and though the trial organizers looked over the sheep pretty well, since nobody was expecting a half-blind sheep, nobody saw her.

When Nop's bunch was released at the top end, three sheep started to graze, but the one-eyed sheep took off down the fence line, followed by a young ewe who admired decisiveness.

It was hard going from the get-go—that one-eyed sheep was polarized between fight and flight. Sometimes, losing sight of the dog behind her, she'd bolt, and when Nop headed her, she'd defy him. Time and time again, Nop regrouped his sheep, but he couldn't get far.

"Time," the scorekeeper called. Nop came off the course and clambered stiffly into the big water tub and lay there, his fur wafting in the water.

Lewis whooshed water over Nop's back. The fellow watching wasn't saying anything, had his arms folded, so Lewis didn't say anything either, just cooled Nop down. The fellow had dark black hair and a sallow complexion and his cowboy shirt was going on its third day.

When Nop stepped out of the tub he was so whipped he didn't shake himself dry. "I'm Ransome Barlow," the fellow said. "We never met. I got that Bute dog that's tearin' up the circuit this year. Dog had three other owners this side of the ocean. Wasn't nobody could do anything with him."

"I'll be watching for him," Lewis said. Nop gave a feeble shake, another one.

"I heard a lot about this Nop dog. I wished I could have seen him in his prime."

"Where you from, Mr. Barlow?"

"No need to call me Mister. I come from Johnson City, Iowa. That Hope dog of Penny's, he out of Nop?"

"Yes, sir."

"Don't have to call me sir, neither. I vote Democrat."

"You'll excuse me, Mr. Barlow. I got to put my dog up."

The gent didn't budge. "When that spotty-faced ewe broke off like that, why didn't you call the dog on, show her who was runnin' the show?"

Lewis said, "She was part blind. Nop was handling her best he could."

"I fancy a bit more control on a dog."

Back in the motor home, Lewis toweled Nop dry and tied him in the shade.

Beverly gave him a pat and Nop rolled on his back for a scratch. She said, "I thought Nop did real good."

"Just the luck of the draw."

By four o'clock, Roger Schroeder and Don were holding down first place with 92 points (they'd lost points on the lift and pen), and Bruce Fogt and Molly were scant points behind.

Ransome Barlow strutted to the post, hips pushed out in front of him like a teenager on a Saturday night. At his side, his dog Bute was pure tension, like he might do something dangerous.

Some people said Ransome Barlow's Bute was "mechanical"—certainly Ransome commanded him every step of the way, whistles tumbling over each other like a mountain stream. And the black brute took the commands too, every one, step to the left, half step to the right, and Ransome steered that dog through the course, but Bute was so keen Ransome kept the brakes on, whistling his "Take Time" and his "Steady" and his "Stand."

Lewis turned to a Texas handler. "Man can handle a dog," he said.

"You betcha," the Texan replied.

As soon as he finished, Ransome left the course. He ignored the cooling-off tub, chained Bute up, and returned as they posted his score: 95½. His only remark was, "Where'd he get that half point from?"

And that's how the long afternoon went. People ran dogs, talked dogs, watched dogs. Those who'd run well were modestly proud, those who ran badly found excuses.

When Penny came on the course with Hope, the light was falling, and out in the sagebrush those dim brownish gray shapes were sheep. She spoke to the dog at her side for a long time, whispering.

Of the dogs that ran that day, Hope was the youngest, but you wouldn't know it by the way he went out, strong and quick. He started coming in tight on his outrun but Penny whistled him out.

In the horse trailer, the judge murmured, "That'll be a point," and the secretary deducted one point from Penny's 100.

Penny whistled Hope down, right at twelve o'clock, which looked neat, but the sheep were heavy to the left and they drifted that way.

"Two off the lift," the judge said.

Penny asked Hope to come around and the dog brought the sheep very nicely down the course, except for a hesitation at the fetch gates. ("Two points," the judge noted.) At the turn, Hope came around on his sheep nicely, balanced so perfectly the judge turned to his secretary and asked, "Do you know his breeding?" and the secretary said, "He's not an Arizona dog."

Hope had one of his ears forward, the other cocked back for Penny's command. The sheep hit the drive gate dead center and Hope knew Penny's whistle was too urgent, but took it against his better judgment.

"Two points off," the judge remarked. "No, make that a point, she's got control again."

Hope settled his sheep, and, nicely, they crossed the course, bang through the crossdrive gate, and this time, the command was timed perfectly. Penny waited until the sheep were near (horned ewe in the lead) before she swung the pen gate wide and stepped behind it. Hope pushed on and Penny told Hope, "lie down," which he did, relieving pressure, and the horned ewe had a moment to think just when she shouldn't have been given one.

"The dog was right," the judge said. "I'll have a half point for that."

Hope saw that the world was getting away from him, that

things were going to break bad, and stood without command and simply leaned forward and the horned ewe thought, Oh, dear, Oh dear, and went into the pen and her mates followed.

Penny dragged the gate shut: one minute remaining.

When the sheep came into the shedding ring Penny would try to take off the last sheep in line.

Crook in hand, Penny stood on one side of the sheep and Hope slipped around to the other.

The sheep got strung out single file, and Hope cocked himself to come through, but Penny feared the sheep were getting away and stopped the lead sheep from escaping. So they bunched up again.

"How much time has she?" the judge asked.

"Thirty seconds."

"What a shame."

The sheep were a solid lump of wooley sheepflesh, swirling, and though Penny tried to separate them, they were like commuters jammed in a subway car, nothing could break them apart. Penny jabbed at the sheep with her stick, pushed her knee at them but unlike the Dead Sea, they did not part and when finally, in desperation, she called Hope in, the dog charged and the sheep broke, but Hope cut off two sheep instead of one, and before Penny could decide what to do, the judge called, "Time."

It was like coming out of a darkened movie theater on a bright Arizona afternoon: reality rushed in, hot and painful. Sweat was running into her eyes, her shirt was prickly against her skin, Hope's tongue hung out, there was grass under Penny's feet, spectators, gray-blue sky overhead. Next slide, please.

Faces, handlers she knew, said words to her as she came off

the field, and Penny said, "uh-huh, thanks," and at the cooling tub, Hope jumped in, lapped his fill, shook, said, "Thee and I need to talk," and took off. Penny felt a cramp and wondered if she was getting her period, but it had been months since she had a period and she followed Hope to the pickup. She filled his food bowl but he ignored it.

"Alright. So, what'd I do wrong?" she asked.

Hope shrugged, "If thee cannot do thy work, seek help from one who can."

—— ❧ ——

March 5, Final go-round, Tuscon, Arizona
Judge: Bill Berhow, Lavina, Montana

60 Open dogs went to the post

1. Ransome Barlow	Bute	95½
2. Ted Johnson	Craig	89
3. Penny Burkeholder	Hope	86
4. Betty Maddux	Mirk	86
5. Bruce Fogt	Molly	84

"I'D FEEL FOOLISH wearing one of those string ties," Lewis Burkeholder said.

"I never thought I'd ever see you wearing any tie," Beverly said. "You look nice."

The Burkeholders had showered in the RV, though they couldn't run the water as long as they did at home. Beverly put on the light blue dress she wore to her cousin's wedding, and Lewis wore his corduroy sport jacket, red and blue tie, western shirt, and chinos. Out here everybody wore a Texas hat—hat'd be okay. Beverly fastened the safety clip of the antique silver and amethyst bracelet Lewis bought her for her birthday two years ago. Happier times.

"You know, Beverly," Lewis said, "if I was to retire, sell out, we could take this thing on the road. Why, we could go all the way down to Mexico."

"Lewis, don't be silly. Neither you nor me knows a word of Mexican."

They went to dinner in Penny's pickup: Penny, Ethel Harwood, Lewis, and Beverly. Hope rode on the floorboards under Lewis's feet and wasn't happy with the forest of legs surrounding him.

"Good thing this is an old truck," Lewis said. "I'd hate to fit four people in the cab of a new one."

Penny said, "Hope, you hush up. Don't you get to growling."

Beverly said, "Lewis, would you please put your arm behind us. I'm sure Ethel won't mind."

"Over there," Ethel said. "Penny get in the left lane."

The Conquistador was done in mission style. The ceiling beams were dyed and distressed, the lobby furniture had thick legs and slab tops, and an original oil painting of conquistadors hung over the registration desk. Beverly got goose bumps on her arms and wished she'd thought to bring a sweater. The hostess made a point of checking the reservation book before saying, "Yes, Mr. Burkeholder, I think we can fit you in."

Ethel Harwood said, "Course you can. There's not ten people in this barn."

The menus were the size of road atlases. The waitress who filled their water glasses had Indian features, but when she introduced herself her accent wasn't any different from the Arizona drawl they'd been hearing all day.

Ethel said, "Good evening, we've been out all day in the sun and I am blasted thirsty. Gin and tonic for me." Penny said no she didn't want anything and Beverly said maybe a glass of white wine and Lewis, who rarely drank anything, had a recollection of a Jimmy Stewart movie he'd seen as a youngster, where Stewart's family gathered together for an occasion and Lewis said, "This is a family reunion for us, Miss. I think we'd like a bottle of champagne."

When the waitress offered Lewis the wine list, he grinned, "I wouldn't know a good one from a bad one. Bring us the one people usually order, if it's not too dear." And, to Penny, leaning toward her, "That was a good run you had going today. Too bad about the shed."

Beverly said, "My cousin Irma got married again last month. Third time. A dentist, has a practice in Stephen's City. They're off to Bermuda for their honeymoon. Ethel, you ever get to Bermuda?"

Ethel hadn't, though she'd been to Britain for the International Sheepdog Trials. Lewis had questions about the sheepdog trials.

Ethel Harwood ordered the Mexicali platter, Beverly wanted fish sticks and the salad bar, Penny said she wasn't very hungry, just the salad bar, please, and Lewis went for the surf and turf.

With so few diners, the salad bar hadn't been picked over and Beverly took some of those tiny hot peppers that you never find on salad bars in Virginia.

Lewis said, "The sunsets out here are really something."

Ethel said, "Is your fish alright?"

Beverly told Penny about weddings and divorces, deaths and births among the farm people she'd grown up with. Penny picked at her salad.

Ethel talked about the Texas Olympics, how it had rained

so hard. Everybody expected Herbert Holmes would win with Dave, but Ransome Barlow never made a mistake.

Penny said, "Ransome's the best dog man in the country."

Lewis said, "That Bute dog is too hard. I wouldn't want to send him after young lambs."

Penny said, "He's a whale of a trial dog."

Lewis said, "Trials aren't everything."

The waitress said, "Sir, is everything alright? You haven't touched your dinner."

Lewis said, "I guess my eyes were bigger than my stomach, ha, ha."

Beverly said, "I'll have a little more of that champagne, please. My isn't this good?"

Lewis put down his fork. "You comin' home any time soon?" he asked his daughter.

Penny set her fork down too.

Beverly said, "Penny, I know you been through a lot . . ."

Ethel Harwood said, "They didn't put enough lime in my gin and tonic. I think I'll go ask about it."

Lewis waited until Ethel was gone before he said, "You could move back to our house. There's no sense paying two electric bills."

Penny pushed her plate away. "Hope came sixth today, Daddy, and he's good enough to win if I get my act together. It isn't the same as it was with you and Nop. Hope and me, we've been through a lot together . . ."

Lewis stiffened. "I do believe I have an idea what a dog can mean to a person . . ."

"Don't you see, Daddy? Don't you see? I'm concentrating now and I only have the one thing on my mind. When I'm out on that trial field, I could be anybody, I don't have to be me.

Hope and dog trialing—they take up all my space, and at night, when I lay down, I'm too tired to dream."

Beverly said, "Honey, it's just that we miss you so."

"Mama, last week a whole afternoon went by when I didn't think about Lisa, not one time. I'm getting better, Mama. I'll come home when I'm well again."

Lewis swallowed. For a time he studied the back of his rough hands, lying on the white tablecloth. "If you put too much pressure on your sheep they'll bunch up. Back off them and they'll open a space for your dog. That Hope is a natural shedding dog if you give him half a chance."

Lewis caught the waitress's eye and ordered coffee. When she came back, Ethel Harwood had a glass of ice tea. She said she didn't want another bite she was so full, no, nobody wanted any dessert.

Ethel and Beverly talked, remembering great dogs and their handlers. Ada Karrasch, the first woman handler, who always competed in a red pants suit and a red cowboy hat and when she and her dogs beat the men, they wouldn't talk to her. Ethel remembered Lewis Pence and Pope Robertson and Dewey Joontz.

"Doug Whittenaur, remember him? Whatever happened to him?"

Lewis shrugged. "I heard he went into bankruptcy."

Ethel remembered when Penny won the Kentucky Bluegrass, with the Stink dog.

"Stink was a great dog," Lewis said, then called for the check. "I'd like to get an early start tomorrow."

Ethel said, "You're not going to run again?"

Lewis shook his head. "Old Nop can't make up the points

he lost today. No sense putting him through it. I believe we'll just go on home."

Penny said, "I wish . . . I . . ."

Lewis inspected the check and whistled. "Didn't I ask for a low-priced champagne? I hope the kitchen crew gets more pleasure out of it than we did."

It was chillier driving home and the windows were rolled up and it was cramped and Ethel Harwood's perfume wasn't the same as Beverly's and Lewis wished he hadn't bothered to put on aftershave. Saturday drunks raced by in the fast lane and Lewis thought if they got hit, it'd be the end of them, four humans and the dog on the floorboards.

He thought it probably wouldn't matter much, that the sudden extinction of a truckload of travelers and their dog wouldn't slow traffic for longer than it took to get the junk off the road. Car after car, fast-food joint after chain motel—Lewis badly wanted to be outside the city limits, to be where he belonged.

The next day, Hope lost three points at the shed, but that was good enough for a third—a fancy plaque and $480. Ransome Barlow won the gold engraved belt buckle, and $800. Ransome said, "That isn't a bad dog there. If you could teach him how to shed."

"It's me who don't know how," Penny said. "I was thinking we could save some money if we traveled together."

THE SALESMAN SAID, "Your Dodge's got a hundred five on it. Five hundred's as high as I can go. I can't wholesale it for that."

Penny said, "You gave Ransome fifteen hundred for his

truck and my motor was completely rebuilt not three months ago. Somebody's gonna get a lot of good miles out of that Dodge."

The salesman wore a short-sleeved polyester shirt, which was pulling away from its buttons. "Why don't you keep it then?"

Ransome leaned against the fender of the Ford 250 they were trading for. He watched cars and trucks go by.

Penny said, "The idea was that Ransome and me would trade in both our trucks for one newer one. You got any idea what kind of money we make at sheep dog trials?"

"I'm allergic to dogs," the salesman said.

Didn't slow her a jot. "You make money if you're first or second. Third is break-even and fourth don't pay for the gas. Why do you think me and him are traveling together?"

The salesman sighed. "Miss, I don't know why you're traveling together. That Ford's a good truck. Thirty thousand miles plus a three-month warranty."

"We got no use for your warranty, won't be back in Tucson until next year. How much without it?"

"I'll give you fifty more for no warranty, fifty for your rebuilt motor—"

"That motor was three hundred dollars!"

"Yeah, but you can't see it. Customer look at your truck ask me how come an old truck's only showing five K on the odometer and I tell 'em about your rebuilt motor and they say, 'Sure, sure. What do you want for the Toyota over there?'" Across the highway a new Porsche waited for a break in traffic before it swept away with a mutter as sweet as anything in the world. "How old are you?" the salesman asked.

"Twenty-six."

"I would have guessed you for older. Six fifty, no warranty, take it or leave it."

Ransome didn't help as she moved her sleeping bag and
clothes and Hope's dog bowls and her feminine articles into the
new truck's camper. "Hope rides up front," she said.

March 12, Bascomb, Texas
Judge: Ralph Pulfer, Quincy, Ohio

38 Open dogs went to the post

1. Orin Barnes	Sioux	91	
2. Ransome Barlow	Bute	90	
3. E.B. Raley	Kim	88	
4. Red Oliver	Roy	88	(Decided on outwork)
5. Herbert Holmes	Dave	87	

IN THE WEEK they'd been traveling together the nicest thing Ransome said to her was, "If you keep jabbering I won't fall asleep at the wheel."

Nicest thing she'd said to him was after he came off the course at Bittersweet: "That'll be the run to beat." Meanest thing she did to him was taking her sleeping bag and air mattress outside every night and lying beside the truck, and once when it rained, she scooted underneath and spent the night beneath the drive train. Meanest thing he said to her was outside of Oklahoma City when she asked to stop at a rest area an hour and a half after they'd gassed up. "You don't hold your water too good do you?"

ARDMORE OKLAHOMA RANCH DOG TRIAL

March 26, Ardmore, Oklahoma
Judge: Ted Johnson, Shorter, Alabama

27 Open dogs went to the post

1. Ralph Pulfer	Sweep	93
2. Dodie Green	Soot	90
3. Earnest Coggins	Moss	89
4. Ransome Barlow	Bute	88
5. Penny Burkeholder	Hope	84

"I T W A S Y O U who hit that curb and ruined the tire," Penny said. "I don't see why I got to pay half the new one."

"Because you still owe me and unless you pay half we're on the thumb."

"What about Penn Y Careau? Is it a good trial?"

He shrugged. "Do you like Florida?"

"I've never been to Florida."

"Course is alright. Sheep are a little ragged."

"When was the last time you changed your socks?"

"What's the matter with my socks?"

I-66, east of Tulsa. The radio played Willie Nelson singing "Stardust." Penny set her hat low over her eyes. The glare off the hood was awful.

"Ask Hope. He's the one got to lie beside them."

"Well hell . . . Well hell . . . You ain't exactly Miss dainty and feminine yourself, you know."

"I wash out my things every night. Might be you could do the same."

103

Hope shifted himself as Ransome kicked out of his boots and dragged his socks off, one at a time, and tied them to the outside mirror.

"Damn things can air dry."

JEFFERSON COUNTY FAIR

❧

April 9, Tangiers, Ohio
Judge: Bruce Fogt, Sidney, Ohio

24 Open dogs went to the post
1. Ransome Barlow   Bute   89
2. Kathy Knox   Scot   88
3. Penny Burkeholder   Hope   88 (Decided on outwork)
4. George Conboy   Raina   85
5. Dick Bruner   Mac   83

ROY'S DOG FOOD CLASSIC

❧

April 23, Shorter, Alabama
Judge: Ralph Pulfer, Quincy, Ohio

1. Ransome Barlow   Bute   93
2. Ted Johnson   Craig   92
3. Earnest Coggins   Moss   90
4. Marilyn Fischer   Connie   89
5. Leroy Boyd   Bess   87

RANSOME GESTURED with his free hand as they rolled across the Mississippi Delta. "You got to give the sheep more room at the pen."

"How'm I going to give them room when I can't let go of the pen rope?"

The air rolling through the window was like a blast furnace but it was perfumed too. The first two weeks of May, all the Delta blooms, the cotton, the soybeans, the spiky plantains along the roadside.

"I already told you that," he said.

Ransome would give her answers, but was unwilling to repeat or elaborate them. Sometimes, rarely, she could get him to explain by coming at him from another angle: "What are the sheep thinking during the pen? What about the lead sheep, where do I want my lead sheep to be?" But many of Ransome's answers were as informative as Zen koans. They did better discussing judging—so long as it wasn't what the judge thought of her run or his.

"Why'd Ted Johnson lose a point at the pen? His sheep didn't circle the pen or anything."

"Those were easy penning sheep and they balked for a long time in the opening. Sheep like that, the judge is going to hit you every point he can."

"But that means he'll be tougher on the good runs than the bad."

"Course he will. Judge has got to protect himself. He always got to leave room for the perfect dog."

~

May 6, Johnston, Mississippi
Judge: Bruce Fogt, Sidney, Ohio

24 Open dogs went to the post

1. Kathy Conner	Meg	89
2. Ted Johnson	Jan	88
3. Ransome Barlow	Bute	87
4. Leroy Boyd	Bess	84
5. Penny Burkeholder	Hope	82

"I don't like it, all your frillies flapping around in the camper back there."

"Ransome, it's night. Nobody can see them. I got to dry them out or I'll have nothing clean. Maybe it don't bother you to go without clean underwear, but I can't stand it. It makes me feel like I got sand fleas all over my body."

The truck windshield rushed through a bug blizzard. Insects fluttered to either side or kamikazied straight in. Every few miles Ransome ran the windshield washer and smeared two semicircles of visibility. Hope whimpered in his sleep.

"It's alright, honey," Penny said and stroked Hope's head. He didn't wake but he stopped twitching. "I don't know how you can stand it, day after day in the same clothes."

"I got my trial shirt. Don't wear that for longer than twenty minutes a day and I hang it up soon as I come off. How many times twenty minutes go into twenty-four hours?"

"It's a good thing it ain't winter."

They rode down the road for twenty miles before Ransome asked, "Why's that?"

"We'd have to travel with the windows shut."

May 13, Jonestown, Ohio
Judge: Tom Wilson, Gordonsville, Virginia

21 Open dogs went to the post

1. Ransome Barlow	Bute	94
2. Kent Kuykendall	Bill	90
3. Bruce Fogt	Molly	84
4. Florence Wilson	Kate	83
5. Penny Burkeholder	Hope	82

THEY WERE COMING OUT of Columbus on I-95 when they hit the dog. The median strip is narrow there and the dog had dodged onto it under the snout of a Kenilworth and maybe he was hysterical or maybe he thought he had nothing to lose because he kept coming. Ransome jerked the wheel and stuff broke loose inside the camper but there was this solemn thud on the side of the truck and that was that.

"Ransome, he's trying to get up." Penny had her eyes glued to the rearview mirror. "Ransome, stop!"

"How the hell I'm going to do that!" They were around the bend and the Freightliner on their butt pulled out to pass and blatted his airhorn, in sympathy or derision.

"We've got to go back." They passed a sign: DEGRAFF 14.

Ransome hit the hazard blinkers and slowed and took AU-THORIZED VEHICLES ONLY. When he pulled back into traffic stuff shifted around in the camper again.

"Ransome, I think he was a Border Collie."

"How the hell you know that?"

"Look, there he is. He's got back to the median."

He was a black and tan smooth-coated bitch with a broad head. She hadn't been eating well before she wandered onto the interstate: her ribs quivered under her skin like steel guitar strings. Half the hair was off her tail, like she'd been flayed. She was just lying there.

The median was ten feet of dead grass and soda pop bottles. A Kentucky Fried Chicken "Bucket of Chicken" lay behind the dog, a Mello Yello bottle a few feet ahead. It was hot, and every time a sixteen wheeler came by the air billowed and sucked.

"Ransome, what are you doing?" The bitch was panting hard, licking her lips, her eyes followed Penny's every move.

"I got me a tire iron behind the seat. Christ, Penny, this is a mess. I like to keep things tidy." He held the tire iron in his hand like the familiar tool had turned strange. "You scoot back in the truck. This won't take but a moment."

"Just what do you think you're doing?"

"I'm putting this poor bitch down, is what I'm doing. What do you think I'm doing. You want to drive away and leave her? Go on. You don't have to watch."

"Ransome, she isn't hurt that bad. Look, her eyes are open."

"She's no account and she's hurt bad. I'll be doing her a favor."

A double trailer rig roared by. The air was thick with its passage. "She must have been terrified. Ransome, I'm asking you."

And Penny looked at him and the hurt bitch looked at him and Ransome said, "Won't be the first dumb thing I've done in my life," and went back to the truck and got a dog crate. He knelt beside her and said, "Alright, girl, this won't hurt a bit," and tied his checked neckerchief around her muzzle.

"She doesn't need that?"

"She's hurt, scared. She don't know us from Adam. Lift her careful, don't twist her now."

The dog was panting like there wasn't enough air in the world as they slid the crate in beside Bute, who pawed his crate door to be let out. "You cut that out," Ransome said.

When they were rolling again, Ransome said, "I don't know if DeGraff has got a dog pound."

"Dog pound'll just kill her."

"What in the hell do you want to do? She's not your dog. You wouldn't want her if she was healthy. She's probably not even a Border Collie, some kind of shepherd mix."

"She's the spitting image of Tom Lacy's Rip, same muzzle."

"What if she is? She's not trained. You don't know anything about her. The world is full of useless dogs nobody wants."

"Are you always so hard? What made you so hard?"

Ransome shut up. He knew to a dollar how much money Penny had, every prize she'd won. She'd barely scraped up enough to send her entry check to the Blue Ridge Trial and she was dead broke. Ransome had a couple hundred dollars in the bank and as much in his wallet, and he'd been paying their joint expenses. He couldn't remember the last time she'd paid for a tank of gas.

Ransome wished he was traveling alone. "You ever hear the story of the dog handler who goes to help the rancher load his calves? Well, his dogs don't know anything and the handler knows less and all morning there's cows running this way and that and everybody hollerin' and everything gets done shouldn't have. Finally the rancher looks at the dog man and says, "I'd like to thank you for comin' out here to help me. Having you and your dogs is like having two good men stay home.""

"I wish she'd stop howling," Penny said.

The Mint Springs Veterinary Clinic had loading dock and chutes around back for large animals, and that's where Ransome backed in. "You go tell 'em what we got," Ransome said. "I'll wait with the truck."

The bitch stopped howling when he opened the camper. There was blood coming out of her mouth and she was swallowing it down.

Maybe that was the secret. Keep it all inside, give nothing away.

The bitch's eyes were desperate.

Ransome said, "I didn't cause your trouble. Wasn't me turned you loose to forage on your own," but the words didn't make him feel better. "I ain't got the extra for this," he said. "There's plenty of men who got extra, but I don't." The bitch swallowed more blood.

The boom of a steel door and footfalls over a concrete floor and the vet was wearing a white smock and his assistant was wearing a green one. The assistant pushed a stainless steel trolley.

"Just leave her in the crate. We'll take her that way." The vet looked at Ransome.

"She ain't my dog," Ransome said. "I hit her on the interstate."

Penny came around from the front, hurrying.

"But you'll be responsible," the vet said. The vet was a young man with blond hair and a darker reddish moustache. He was about Ransome's age. Ransome wondered how much he made in a year.

As the vet tech wheeled her away, the bitch started howling again. Things, Ransome thought, were out of hand.

"I'll be responsible," Penny said.

"We'll do what we can," the vet said, nodded briskly, and disappeared.

Ransome moved the truck over to the end of the lot where Bute and Hope could stretch their legs. Penny had one foot on the bumper and a distant look on her face. "What are you going to do with her if she pulls through?" Ransome asked.

She shook her head. "I can't stand any more senseless dying."

Ransome took a dip of snuff. "Your husband—was he a dog man?"

"Mark wasn't much of a hand with animals. Oh, he could work a chute or corral, and after Nop brought the sheep, Mark knew what to do, but he never was real interested. He knew grasses—we'd take walks through the meadows and he'd point out the different bluegrasses, the clovers, the ironweed, pigweed, purpletop, blue stems . . ."

"You and him, you . . ."

"What got you so curious, all of a sudden."

112

"I was just asking . . ."

"Yeah. Well, Mark took my daughter for a drive in the rain when it was pouring down so hard he could hardly see and then he got in an accident and couldn't get Lisa out of the truck and she drowned. Any other questions?"

"What makes you so hard?"

She looked at him sharply and then the tears came to her eyes, so he walked over to the grass and called Bute to him. Just like that hurt bitch in the vet clinic, Bute was busy dying. He was just going about it more gradually. Bute was five now. Roy was still winning trials for John Templeton when he was eleven, but that was real unusual. Maybe Ransome should look for a new young dog to start. "I never had no family to speak of," he said. "My dad ran out on us. You know that Bruce Springsteen song about everybody's got a hungry heart? I'm sorry you lost your family. I never figured I was much account, so I always figured to put all I had into doing one thing and I'd get that right. I never thought anybody else was more account than me and they never had the one thing to do right."

"You're a hell of a dog man. What do you want more than that?"

Ransome shrugged. He thought to say something about a wife, a family, a home, but, the truth was he wasn't sure he wanted those things though he knew he was supposed to want them. "It'd be nice if that bitch lived. I never ran over her with the tires; it was a glancing blow."

"It's what I admire about you. Sometimes when you're out on the trial field, you can take my breath away."

"Yeah. Well sometimes I get lucky. What are you going to do after the National Handlers' Finals?"

"Polish my trophy."

"No really?"

Penny watched Hope, who was rolling in the grass. "It's kind of like praying," she said softly. "You don't know what you're going to do until after you know if God is going to answer."

"I come second last year. It's just a trial. Bigger. Outrun's nearly a mile."

"Isn't anything you can't make small. The World Series is just a bunch of overgrown boys playing ball and the same jerks want to be President of the United States wanted to be president of the senior class. My Lisa . . . there's millions of kids died in worse pain, plenty kids didn't have the life she did. How about you and me? Two misfits who'll put sixty thousand miles on this pickup this year to run in pennyante dog trials. You can look at it that way."

"Come over here, Bute. That's enough foolishness." The vet tech had crossed the tarmac to say that the doctor would see them now.

The corridors of the cavernous building were damp and cold. Big drains in the concrete floors. The operating room was brightly lit, like everything important was concentrated right here. The bitch lay on the steel table on her side with some kind of tube that looked like a vacuum cleaner part way down her throat. Penny never knew a dog's tongue could come out so far. They'd shaved a wide strip of hair and pulled back a flap of belly skin and her innards were inside like aliens in a cave.

"Excuse me," Ransome said and retreated into the hall, and the door hissed shut behind him.

The vet was wearing his mask and his disposable gloves, and the front of his uniform was bloody from table top height to his ribcage. "It doesn't look good."

"Poor bitch. The poor little bitch . . ."

"I'm afraid her spleen is ruptured and there's substantial damage to the liver too."

"You want me to say we should kill her."

"If I patch her back together she'll live a couple days, in pain, getting weaker and weaker."

Penny shook her head. "I'm not up to this. Poor bitch is so alone. Wait a minute. Let me ask my partner."

Ransome was at the back door drawing big drafts of air. "Sorry," he said, "I see blood and I get squeamish. I might pass out."

"Well, you got to go back in there and tell that vet what to do."

He looked at her for a moment. "If I start to go gray faced, you steer me out of there."

And so the lost bitch died, issued out of life with more human gentleness than she had known during her life, with the gentle hand on her neck of a hard man who couldn't look at her and a woman's voice in her ears, "Poor baby. Good-bye, poor baby, good-bye."

Yes the clinic would dispose of the dog. They had an incinerator. The vet said, "I wish it could have turned out better."

A gray-faced Ransome Barlow said, "Dog wasn't any account anyway," and swallowed.

The vet said, "I'll work for free, but I'm going to have to charge you the medications and incineration."

Penny wrote him a check for sixty dollars, which meant

her check to the Bluegrass Trial would bounce when they cashed it.

Outside, Ransome took a deep breath of air and set his hat straight across his forehead. "Would have been cheaper with the tire iron," he said.

"Ransome," she said, "I won't say it's been fun traveling with you, but it sure has been *interesting*. Know what I mean?"

━━━━━━━━━━━━━━━━━━ ❧ ━━━━━━━━━━━━━━━━━━

May 21, 1st day, Lady Lake Florida
Judge: Lewis Pulfer, Quincy, Ohio

60 Open dogs went to the post

1. Ralph Pulfer	Ken	87
2. Ransome Barlow	Bute	87 (Decided on outwork)
3. Ethel Conrad	Jan	86
4. Bobby Ford	Yogi	80
5. Quinn Tindall	Shep	79

EVERY MORNING, as soon as Penny stirred, Hope stretched and yawned and went to her sleeping bag and put his nose within a millimeter of her cheek and smelled whether she was awake. If she slept, he grunted and laid back down again. If she was awake, he licked her cheek, just once, and laid down and thumped his tail against her sleeping bag.

While she struggled into her clothes, he sniffed around the area, tail held high, reading all the messages posted since last night. SICK, OLDER DOG, WATCH OUT—one said. YOUNG NERVOUS DOG—BEWARE, said another. YOUNG LADY IN HER PRIME . . . and so forth. He overlapped a few messages of his own. DEVIL-MAY-CARE YOUNG DOG SEEKS LOVE AND ADVENTURE. That was Hope's customary signature.

Some mornings fog coiled among the gypsy encampment, blurring the outlines of the motor homes, the rows of pickup campers. A door would bang open and two or three dogs would hurtle out into the morning, and several would charge straight at Hope in a brusk and determined manner. Hope's hackles would rise and he'd stand fast until the other dogs were quite close before circling them, which is part threat (hindquarters being relatively undefended) and part politeness. The dog who stands straight and doesn't circle is itching for a fight.

Hope knew these dogs. Knew Ethel Conrad's crotchety old Tess and Bill Berhow's joking dog, Nick. Knew Barbara Ligon's quick Mirk and Roy Johnson's devoted Roscoe.

Once the introductions were made, ("And how art thou, this morning?") dogs would provoke a chase and bound away full tilt, under the RV's, around the outskirts of the course, running because they were made for it, created by God for that purpose, and they had the joy of it in their legs, their dogginess in their dodge, their sheer pleasure at a new day.

Suddenly, Hope would be overtaken by a reminder from his own innards that he was full, full to bursting and he'd find a bush or some tall grass where he could squat safe with no one watching him, man or dog.

Though he and Bute traveled together, saw more of each other than any other dog, they weren't pals. When Bute came out of the crate in the pickup, he checked the other dogs' calling cards but was indifferent to all but bitches in heat. Bute's calling card read: BAD TO THE BONE. Once, out in Oklahoma, a young dog, startled by Bute's sudden appearance, lunged at him. Bute couldn't have been more astonished if he'd been hit by a meteor. He ran away and made fifteen yards, encouraging the young dog to a foolish pursuit. Then, he turned and threw the young dog over and held him by the throat and the young dog sobered instantly, the fight light going out of his eyes. "Sorry," he whispered. "Sorry." Bute considered killing him, but killing other dogs was not his work, so with a final growl, he stalked off and returned to the pickup, where Ransome had filled his bowl for breakfast.

From time to time, Hope offered to play with Bute, dropped down into the inviting puppy crouch that means: "After you, Gaston," or "After me, Alphonse," but Bute sneered and went about his business.

Like some humans, Bute came alive at his work, had displaced his soul into work. Once Hope asked Bute what he thought about Ransome: "He is the best there is," Bute said.

Before eight o'clock, the sun would burn off the fog, handlers would gather near the judge to hear his instructions and the faint sound of whistles on the course announced that men were putting out sheep. The dogs were tied beside the vehicles, and all day they'd doze, listening to whistles and commands on the course until their turn came.

PENN Y CAERAU STOCKDOG TRIAL

May 22, 2nd day, Lady Lake Florida
Judge: Lewis Pulfer, Quincy, Ohio

58 Open dogs went to the post

1. Ransome Barlow	Bute	90
2. Ralph Pulfer	Ken	88
3. Quinn Tindall	Shep	87
4. Tom Wilson	Cap	85
5. Ethel Conrad	Jan	84

THE BAND WAS PLAYING Bob Will's old tunes and not too bad either. Fiddle, couple guitars, woman singer—big woman, spangled western shirt hanging loose and a blue cowboy hat. Jo-Jo's, the restaurant where they held the Handlers' Dinner and Dance, had a sign on the front door, SORRY: PRIVATE PARTY TONIGHT, and the narrow dining room was full of dog handlers, dressed up in their best western garb. Ransome Barlow wore a red and black striped body shirt with extremely wide droopy lapels. Ransome's run had been one of those efforts most handlers only dream of. Ransome was no dancer, but tonight he had plenty of willing partners.

One harried waitress was hurrying beer around on trays: keep your shirt on, partner. Yeah, six Buds, yeah.

Earlier, Penny showed up at Ethel Harwood's motor home, with her paper bag of clean clothes. "Ethel, you got enough hot water for me to take a shower? I'm sorry to pester you, but I can't go to the dinner tonight like this."

When the young woman came out, Ethel said, "That was good work out there today. You just had some bad breaks."

"Bad breaks don't buy much gas," Penny said. "Thanks for the shower."

Later, at Jo-Jo's Ethel pushed into Penny's corner and made space for herself. "You don't dance? I'm no dancer myself. Forty years ago, I got smacked in the ankle by a polo mallet, and that's where all my arthritis settled."

"Uh-huh. Well, it's humid here."

"Penny, I can't tell you how much I like that Hope dog. I haven't seen a dog I liked so much since Nop was getting started."

"Funny thing, they give the prize money to all the other

dogs. Oh, Ethel, I'm sorry. I know you're just trying to be nice. This dog trialing has got me about three-quarters crazy. It's like we're standing outside a candy store, it's Christmas and the store's all lit up and other kids go in and out, and me and Hope, we just stand outside. I wish I knew what to do. I can't screw Hope down any tighter. All we do is trial, train and trial, but somehow we never get the breaks. If there's a bad sheep in the draw, you can be sure they'll save it for Hope. We aren't making our entry fees."

"I heard a story once about Hamish Wilson, the Scottish dog man. One night he came home in a rage, BANG the door shut, BANG the dogs put up, and muttered curses all the way to the doorstep. Hamish hears the sound of a front window going up and his youngest sticks her head out and says, 'Bad sheep again, eh, Da?' "

Penny managed a grin.

"Ransome," Ethel said, "you smell just like a blue quarter-horse I owned once. Heck of a horse, but you couldn't ride him once around a training ring without he soaked clear through."

"Yes, ma'am. Penny, you dance?"

Penny shook her head. "I got nothing to celebrate."

"It isn't going to hurt you." He extended a hand.

"Suppose you let me be the judge of that."

Ethel stood up. "Come on, Ransome. I've always wanted to dance the Texas two-step with a champion."

The waitress brought more beer. The Texas handlers proved to be the best dancers, Ralph Pulfer came to the microphone and, in a deep baritone sang "Seven Spanish Angels." Applause was enthusiastic.

The band took a break and Penny found Ransome quaffing a glass of ice tea. "I'd like to go back to the trial grounds," she said. "Hope needs to go out."

"Oh hell, the dancing just started."

"Drop me off. You can come back and dance as much as you want."

Soon as Ransome slid behind the wheel, Penny rolled her window all the way down, though it was a coolish evening with fireflies.

Ransome shot her a look. "What's the matter with you. You don't like to have a good time?"

"Ransome, I'm broke. I can't pay my share."

"Luck of the draw, honey." Ransome shrugged. "I'll carry you through the Blue Ridge. Got me a nice check today, fifteen hundred dollars."

Penny thought to say she wasn't his honey, but couldn't look a gift horse in the mouth. At the trial grounds, they let their dogs run around to do their business.

"What was you before you got into the dogs?" Ransome asked.

"Nothing," Penny said. "Hope. Stay out of that! I don't want you rolling around!" She pulled her sleeping bag out of the back of the truck.

"You don't have to do that," Ransome said. "It's softer in the camper, no rocks or nothin'."

She laid out her air mattress, laid her sleeping bag on it, just so.

"Well how about it?"

"How about what?"

"I said you could sleep inside."

"Ransome, I like you as well as I like any man, which isn't

much. I've got a bad attitude." And Penny told Ransome about P.T. and Marvin, the cowboys who'd tried to rape her that January night in Texas. She thought Jack Dickerson knew who they were and she didn't understand why he wouldn't say so. "That's three men," Penny said, "who ain't got anything better to do than treat me like dirt."

WAGGIN' TAILS RANCH TRIAL

May 28, Marcus, South Dakota
Judge: Bill Berhow, Lavina, Montana

26 Open dogs went to the post

1. Bud Boudreau	Patches	88	
2. Dorrance Eikamp	Blue	87	
3. Pat Shannahan	Hannah	87	(Decided on outwork)
4. Roger Culbreath	Trim	86	
5. Bud Boudreau	Cap	85	
26. Ransome Barlow	Bute	Disqualified (grip)	

RANSOME LEANED FORWARD to peer through the rain-streamed windshield. "I never in my life saw a judge like that," he said. "That wasn't a grip at the pen. Bute just nudged that ewe."

"He nudged her with his teeth," Penny said. "That judge was right."

A hundred miles later, Penny said, "What's wrong with you?"

Five hundred miles later, Penny said, "You must be getting tired. If you want, I can drive."

123

Eight hundred miles later, she said, "Suit yourself."

Two thousand six hundred miles later, the sun was just coming over the Blue Ridge. The corn and alfalfa in Shenandoah Valley were wet and glistening with dew. Penny thought to say something about how beautiful it was but there was no point. "Next time we stop for gas," she said, "I'll want to pee."

BLUE RIDGE (1ST TRIAL IN VIRGINIA TRIPLE CROWN)

June 3, 1st day, White Post, Virginia
Judge: Tom Wilson, Gordonsville, Virginia

62 Open dogs went to the post

1. Penny Burkeholder	Hope	96
2. Bruce Fogt	Molly	92
3. Nathan Mooney	Max	90
4. Amanda Milliken	Boy	89
5. Beverly Lambert	Lark	88

THE VIRGINIA TRIPLE CROWN is the most important sheepdog trial series on the East Coast, and the best dog handlers in the United States try to get there.

The first weekend is the prettiest trial, the Blue Ridge, always held on a hilltop with an outrun down into a bowl. The sheep are barbadoes, which tend to be extremely flighty in the morning and docile—some say too docile—in the afternoon. With sheep this workable, top scores are unusually high, well over ninety points, and some judges alter the course, install chutes or races to make the course more difficult and, not incidentally, the judge's job easier.

Washington Post Weekend had announced the trial, and

125

hundreds of city people have come out this day to watch the brilliant dogs, have a day in the country, picnic on the grass. With Instamatics, they gather around the water tubs at the end of the course where the dogs who've just finished flop and lap and cool their parts and the photographers get splashed when the dogs shake themselves.

Penny was watching Kathy Knox with Scot. "Kathy," she muttered, "call him in or you're going to miss that gate."

"Got you talking to yourself, uh? You know what they say about that."

"Hullo, Oren. What are you doin' up north? Haven't you got work back in Texas?"

"Oh, I had a pen of purebred lambs entered in the Eastern Stud Ram Show. This trial wasn't far away. How you doing?"

She turned back to the course. "I knew she should flank that dog."

"I didn't know you came from a famous sheepdog family. Folks speak awful high of your daddy."

"Daddy would make eight, ten trials a year. One year he'd qualified for the National Finals, Nop wasn't but six years old, and Dad didn't go out because he was fall planting wheat and didn't have time."

"Well," Oren drawled, "I s'pose there's more money in wheat than sheep dog trialing. Can I buy you a hamburger or something?"

Penny owed Ransome five hundred dollars. Ransome said he'd let it go to a thousand, but then he'd take a half share in Hope. Penny hadn't won any real money since her third at Tangiers, Ohio. She wasn't thinking about the future, resolutely kept it unthought of, but Penny had to catch up here at the Triple Crown or quit the circuit, go home with her tail between her legs. Ransome didn't win enough to feed two. Ransome could have done paid demonstrations and handler's clinics, but usually turned them down. A couple paid clinics would have suited Penny to a T, but nobody invites losers to teach.

Penny and Hope were slated to run right after lunch, which is nearly the worst slot, after the sheep have already run once and got themselves hot and aggravated.

Oren found Penny out behind the parked cars, Hope dashing here and there checking other dogs' calling cards.

"Hasn't put on much weight has he?"

"Hope's fit. Thanks for the burger." But at the first bite of the red meaty thing, the smell overwhelmed her. She hadn't had a thing to eat all day, but this drooly, greasy meat pulsed in her mouth, and she swallowed, swallowed again. "Here take this."

"You all right?"

She shook her head, gulped Coca-Cola, washed the clot into her stomach where she could forget about it. Another gulp. "I can't eat anything until I come off the course," she said. "I'm sorry, I forgot."

Oren whistled and Hope looked at him. "I'm sure the dog will like it," he said.

"Don't feed my dog," Penny snapped, and at Oren's puzzlement she said, "Sorry, oh hell, I'm sorry. Please go away. Oren, you know me and you always got along good, but not now. Not *now*." And Penny popped her fingers and the dog came to her, and they walked under the trees into the shade.

The announcer said, "We'd like to welcome you to the Blue Ridge Trial, first trial of the Triple Crown."

Some urban spectators had brought their pet Border Collies

to show them what their trained brothers could do. People sprawled in the grass, or lawn chairs or leaned against the snow fence that bordered the course.

"At the post, Nathan Mooney with Max. Nathan's won this trial in 1988. On deck, Penny Burkeholder with Hope, Kay Pine and Molly in the hole. Handlers please be ready when your name is called."

Eight minutes later, Penny and Hope walked onto the course quietly, Hope peering for the sheep. When they paused, at the handler's post, they gave each other the eye. "You ready?"

"You ready?"

And Penny sent Hope out with a quiet "Whsst" and it was pretty from that moment on: pretty outrun, stop, pretty lift, straight fetch, around nice behind Penny, her speaking so quiet spectators couldn't hear her fifty feet away, pretty drive, through the panels, nice pace across the cross drive, wobble there, but corrected and straight through the gates, good tight turn to the pen and Penny holding the gate until the last minute as the sheep go straight in, like they were on rails and she quick closes the gate. Hope walks the sheep to the shedding ring and Penny settles them, settles them, one ewe drops her head for a bite of grass and "HOPE!" comes in, turns on a dime and the startled sheep watches her companions running away and there's this dog, you see, preventing her from everything she ever wanted and she bleats, stamps her foot, bleats and takes a step back, another and now she can't see her companions at all, all she sees is the dog's eyes, deep enough to drown in.

"That's a shed," the judge calls, and the crowd applauds and whoops and Penny raises her head, dazed, like where did all the people come from? And Hope, concentrating on his sheep, doesn't look up at all. "Shed, Miss," the judge calls again, and Penny lifts her white hat, doesn't quite know what to do with it, puts it back on, sets it straight and Penny calls Hope off and Hope comes to her side. Penny bends and pats him and panting, Hope makes for the water where strangers are waiting to shake Penny's hand and congratulate her. From the tub, Hope looks up at her and says, "Thee and me."

Someone was clasping her back. Somebody was estimating how many points she'd have. And Oren was leaning against somebody's pickup. Penny flushed, looked away, and Hope was already out of the tub, shaking herself, and someone else was working sheep at the handler's stake and Hope had his eye on those.

"Excuse me, I got to put my dog up."

"I'm proud of you," Oren Wright said. He spoke soft so only she could hear.

"Oh," she said, and her eyes misted and she wondered why so many things had to happen all at once, never giving a person a chance to get set for them. "Please, don't be." And she called Hope again, though Hope was right at her heel and no call necessary and he was puzzled because she didn't usually babble and Penny fastened Hope to the pickup and set out a clean dish of water and faced away from the trial course to soft fields yellow with the first blooms of Lespediza and the sky was pale blue all the way to the darker Blue Ridge mountains, and Penny cried.

DINNER THAT NIGHT was barbecue, folding chairs on the farm's front lawn overlooking misty pasture at the foot of the hill, but Penny couldn't have told you what she ate. Although people came up to her to praise her run, to touch some part of what she'd done, she couldn't have named one of them a moment after they were gone from her sight.

Since this was a 'handlers only' dinner, Oren Wright had returned to his motel and Ransome made himself scarce too. Penny was grateful for that.

Penny's heart had swelled until it filled her chest cavity to bursting. Conventional remarks didn't bother her: "You brought that dog along good since I seen you in Tucson," "that was a *real* run you laid down." But there were people who came diffidently near and said, "When that dog of yours came in for the shed, my oh, my . . . ," and a rerun would pass before Penny's mind and she'd say, "Excuse me," and turn and blow her nose into the napkin she clutched in her hand until it disintegrated.

Her hands wouldn't stop shaking and she wished she'd thought to bring her jacket.

In small groups on the lawn, handlers talked softly, drank beer, talked dogs, famous dogs of their youth, dogs in Scotland or Wales, dogs that had just been imported to this country.

Hope rested in the shade of the pickup truck, his nose in the grass, water at one paw, bowl of food at the other. Flies buzzed his untouched food bowl and walked the rim and he ignored them.

He watched the other dogs being exercised and smelled the smoke from the barbecue.

Like Penny, he knew perfectly well he'd done something splendid. Unlike her, however, he didn't think there was anything extraordinary about that, and next morning, first thing, he planned to go out and do it again. This deep satisfaction, the tiredness in his muscles, his mind slowly softening from its grand concentration, was Hope's rational world. Clouds swirled overhead and the fat moon struck through now and again. Motor home doors opened and shut. Though some handlers carried flashlights, the dogs they turned loose for one last romp didn't need them.

Hope recognized the shape coming wearily up the hill and his tail thumped once, twice.

The woman who sat beside him smelled of what she'd eaten, the afternoon's hard sweat, her exultation. "How you doin', honey?"

Hope said he felt fine that today was a good day, would she care to follow him out into the field where all sorts of messages had been collecting.

"Sure," Penny said, and walked into the darkness.

When the moon found a hole in the clouds it arrived like a spotlight, flattening shadows, washing Hope's black and white coat shades of gray.

Hope picked up his feet, sniffed, circled, crouched, scuffed dirt over his own scat, grinning at her, his teeth shining in the moonlight, scuff, scuff, scuff: life was their private joke.

THE SECOND DAY of the Blue Ridge Trial, Penny misjudged the crossdrive panel and two sheep slipped around the outside. Despite that, her run was good enough to come third, behind Herbert Holmes, who'd had a blazing run, and Lyle Boyer, who beat her by a scant point. They finished a little after four. Low scoring handlers spoke about the next trial down the road or the new young dog they had coming on. Handlers who'd done well waited politely for the official tally.

The scorekeeper held the box of ribbons, "In tenth place,

with a score today of 80 and a cumulative score of 168, Beverly Lambert with Lark."

And the judge shook Beverly's hand and congratulated her and the scorekeeper gave her her ribbon and the envelope with her prize checks.

"In ninth place. . . ."

"Nice run, Ransome," someone said.

"Hard luck at the shed," the judge said.

Ransome didn't manage a smile, slipped the envelope with $37.95 into his pocket.

Bruce Fogt fastened his ribbon (5th) to his shirt. Herbert Holmes took his second place overall trophy (a shepherd with Border Collie guarding a lamb) to his camper and Penny asked Oren to hold her trophy (Border Collie with two lambs) while she shook the judge's hand and pocketed four checks:

Best Drive: $20
1st Place, Saturday, $750
3rd Place, Sunday: $300
1st Place Overall: $500

"Oren, I got to talk. No, not here, over there. You're welcome. Oren, you got enough to cash a three-hundred-dollar check?"

Oren pulled his wallet out of his hip pocket and thumbed through it. "I got a hundred ninety if that'll help you. I can get back home on my card."

"Let me have forty-five."

Wordlessly he extended the bills.

The trial organizer was supervising the crew dismantling the scoreboard.

"It's, uh, I got a note from my bank. . . . Apparently, I, uh, overdrew on my account, and, I'm not real sure, but I think that maybe my entry check'll bounce. I'm real sorry about that but here's the money now."

"What would you have done if you hadn't been in the prize list today?" the organizer asked quietly.

"But I was," Penny said, surprised.

June 6 & 7, Shipman, Virginia
Judge: Tom Wilson, Gordonsville, Virginia

1st day: 53 Open dogs went to the post			2nd day: 52 Open dogs went to the post		
1. Barbara Ligon	Mirk	89	1. Penny Burkeholder	Hope	95
2. Penny Burkeholder	Hope	88	2. Ransome Barlow	Bute	90
3. Lyle Boyer	Mick	87	3. Bruce Fogt	Molly	88
4. Candy Kennedy	Coon	85	4. Lyle Boyer	Jock	86
5. Marilyn Fischer	Connie	84	5. Ethel Conrad	Jan	82

THE SECLUSIVAL TRIAL is in the piney woods south of Charlottesville, and the road cuts are red clay. It's scrubby country, and fields are overgrown with white thorn and honey-suckle except for the long green trial field at Seclusival.

Night before, Oren Wright let his show sheep out to graze all night on the trial course. At dawn, Oren asked Penny if she and Hope could put his sheep back in his gooseneck trailer, and a few minutes later that's where they were, surprised to be inside metal walls so quickly. Oren towed the trailer into the shade.

With a sticky donut and a cup of coffee, Oren parked himself in a lawn chair to watch the first dogs. After a bit, he wiped his fingers and licked them and wiped them again. It was chilly, but it'd get hot soon as that sun cleared the trees.

Gangly fellow pulled a chair next to him. Skin tanned so dark it was sun dried. "Name's Barlow," he announced, both hands wrapped around his coffee. No Styrofoam cup for him, he had one of those insulated models said RAIDERS on it.

"Wright," Oren introduced himself. "You're travelin' with Mz. Burkeholder?"

"I been on the road since January. Don't expect to get home until August. Too hot to trial in August. Penny's talking about the Canadian Circuit, then British Columbia. Not much money up there."

"You raise sheep then?"

"I buy a couple dozen, train my dog. Sell 'em when I go on the road. Don't particularly like sheep. If I was raising animals to make money I'd raise hogs. I know some fellows got confinement hog operations. There's some real money in that."

"Once you got your loans paid off. If you don't mind working with sickly animals. If you don't mind doin' factory work at minimum wage and payin' some banker interest for the privilege of doin' it."

Ransome took a sip of coffee. On the course, a dog came in too hard on his sheep and despite his handler's cries, scattered them. "Me and that dog would have words, directly," he announced.

"What's she to you?" Oren asked.

For the first time Ransome Barlow looked him straight in the eye taking Oren's measure. The gaze was so cool it made Oren flush.

"I ain't rightly sure," Ransome said. "I've not come to any

decision about that. You know about her husband and baby girl?"

"Somebody was talking about it at the last trial—. She never told me a thing. She worked for me last winter, six weeks, her and that dog, and she never said a word about it."

"You think it's right—her and that dog? Sometimes I think she thinks better of that damn dog than she does any human being. Of course," Ransome added judiciously, "I got to admit, that dog has been winning some money the last several days. Her and me make a pretty good team. Ain't nobody gonna teach her more about the dogs than me."

"There's more to life than dogs."

"Oh yeah? What? Sheep? Business? Your career? Anything can be as big as you want it to be. Penny ever tell you how that Hope dog kept her from being raped?" Ransome told what Penny had told him, about the two cowboys, P.T. and Marvin. "Those two bastards didn't do her any good. She was half crazy after losing her family, those two made her crazier. That rape's like a sickness with her. She's completely turned against men. You and her. When she was working for you, you ever get it on?"

On the course, a spotty white dog was making a wobbly fetch.

"Will you look at that?" Oren said. "I like to see a dog work like that."

Ransome Barlow spared it a glance. "Shows you don't know nothin' about dogs," he said. "What about it?"

"I don't think that's any business of yours," Oren said, pronouncing it "bidniz" and "your'n."

Oatlands (Final Trial in Virginia Triple Crown)

⌘

June 10 & 11, Leesburg, Virginia
Judge: Tom Wilson, Gordonsville, Virginia

1st day: 65 Open dogs went to the post		
1. Penny Burkeholder	Hope	95
2. Ransome Barlow	Bute	90
3. Nathan Mooney	Max	86
4. Stu Ligon	Tynne	85
5. Pat Buckley	Bart	84

2nd day: 20 Open dogs went to the post		
1. Ransome Barlow	Bute	92
2. Bruce Fogt	Molly	90
3. Nathan Mooney	Max	89
4. Barbara Ligon	Mirk	88
5. Bobby Ford	Yogi	87
20. Penny Burkeholder	Hope	45

Overall winner, Virginia Triple Crown: Ransome Barlow and Bute.
Bruce Fogt and Molly, runner's up.

PENNY RAN LATE THIRD from last on Saturday, after dusk had settled in and most of the spectators had gone. Oatlands is a long narrow field bordered by an avenue of trees on the right and a nasty-looking wall of brush on the left. The smell from the smoke of the handlers' lamb barbecue wafted over the course.

Penny went out and Hope ran and it was quiet and sure and near perfect as a dog ever gets. No mistakes as he brought four flighty Suffolk crosses around the course and dead straight, not a moment's hesitation, into the pen. That's how Hope got his shed too—like he could go on all day making perfect sheds. Soon as the shed was done, Penny called him off and went to him and bent and gave her dog a tremendous hug. "You and me, baby," she murmured into the thick fur of his neck.

137

In her pocket Penny had $450 in checks from Seclusival—
she'd already mailed her Blue Ridge checks to the bank.

"They overcooked their barbecue," Oren Wright said.
"Lamb's all dry and brown."

"It's not much, but it's paid for."

"Well I haven't paid for mine yet and I'll be damned if I'm
going to. There's a steak house down the street from the
motel."

"You in a motel? I could sure use a shower."

So Penny bundled up her dirty clothes and dropped them
at a laundromat and got a hot shower in Oren's motel room
while Oren sat outside, in the truck listening to the radio.
When she came out her hair was still wet. "You didn't need to
wait out here," she said.

He switched off the radio. "Uh-huh. You ready to eat?"

Mitchell's Steakhouse would be crowded later on this Saturday night, but this early, they didn't have to wait for a booth.
No tablecloth, an array of steak sauces. Oren had the blue
cheese dressing and so did Penny. Oren asked what kind of
wine she liked and she said ice tea so he had a Budweiser.

"How'd you make out at the sheep show?" she asked him.

"Not too shabby. Ram lamb was reserve, the yearling ewe
came second. Fellow from Indiana wants twenty replacement
ewes, gate cut, two hundred each, so that'll pay for my trip."

"I didn't know you showed at many sheep shows."

"Oh yeah," he said, because he didn't want to say that he'd
traveled so far just to see her. "Too bad your father couldn't
make it today. Your homeplace—it isn't far from here?"

She clinked her ice tea stirrer through the ice cubes. "I
imagine he's hurt. It's not like I don't love him, but every time
Daddy comes close I start feeling terrible. He'd chain me to

that farm, those old memories. One day I'll be ready to come home, but not yet. Me and Hope, we . . . You know how much I won so far this week? Better'n fifteen hundred dollars. I'm qualified for the National Finals, and if I win tomorrow, I'll be the winner of the Virginia Triple Crown. I'm going to be able to make my own living, on my own terms, beholden to no man."

The waitress brought their steaks on metal platters, warned Penny her platter was real hot, honey, asked did they want ketchup for their fries? Oren would take another beer, Penny was fine with ice tea, thanks.

Oren stayed with his steak until the edge was off his hunger. "You gonna help me out lambing?"

"Oren, this is *June*."

Oren blushed. "Can't farm unless you plan ahead." He wiped his lips, took a sip of beer. People were lined up at the front door, families mostly.

Around them, table talk was a murmur punctuated by the clatter of cutlery, waitresses calling through the serving window.

"The best-laid plans . . . ," Penny began with a smile, but suddenly stalled and looked around the room blankly.

"You all right?"

She swallowed. "Fine." She coughed, wiped her eyes. "Sometimes I look up and see people who aren't there." She forced a smile. "I'll bet you plan so far ahead you have to keep a list to remember all your plans."

"Bingo," he said, softly, his eyes level. "Man with a plan, that's me."

She held his gaze for a moment before consulting her watch. "My laundry'll be dry."

"It won't run off."

The waitress took away their plates and asked did they want any dessert and Oren said he'd like a cup of coffee.

Penny said, "This is the first evening I've been off the trial grounds since I left your place. Either I'm at a trial or on my way to one. This"—she gestured at the room—"is like a foreign country to me."

"You and Hope came a long way."

"Oh that Hope, he's . . . he's the happiest thing ever happened to me. I mean he's honest, you can see it. Once he knows what I want he'd near die to get it done. He trusts me, Oren. I've never done Hope wrong."

Oren poured milk into his coffee. "Aren't you asking a lot of a dog?"

A couple with two young children slid into the booth behind them and the booth walls shook and Penny said softly, "I'm going to be normal again. One day it'll be me and my little family coming out to dinner, some place just like this, and I'll tell the kids they have to finish their dinner before they get the dessert and I'll ask my husband why we don't get out as often as we did before we had the kids. Oh, it'll be swell . . ." She said excuse me and went into the ladies room to wash her face, and when she came back Oren said, "I'd like another cup of coffee but look at all those people waiting. I guess we should go."

"Get a couple cups to go," Penny said. "We can drink them in your room. Oren"—she put a hand on his—"I have to try."

Back at the motel, she stood silently as he unlocked the outer door. Out front somewhere, they heard the howl of tires and a splash of breaking safety glass and somebody's drunken howl. Penny shivered and took Oren's arm. "Everybody's so alone," she said.

The next morning she said she was sorry, she'd tried, but she'd been thinking about a dog they'd run over out in Ohio, just couldn't get it out of her mind.

Oren said he'd like to talk about her husband and daughter. She said she had to get dressed and get back to the trial grounds, this was the championship. He said he wasn't going to give up on her. They drove into Oatlands at noon.

"I walked your dog this morning," Ransome Barlow said. "And watered him. Me and Bute are high with a ninety-six. You'll have to lay down a real run to tie me."

"No problem." Penny didn't meet his eyes as she unfastened her dog. "Come here, Hope! Over here!"

Oren Wright brought Penny's laundry to the truck and slung it inside.

After her turn the day before, Penny needed ninety points to tie Ransome for first place, and that would give her high cumulative for the Virginia Triple Crown.

It was Penny's first year on the circuit, most everybody respected her father, Lewis, and the handlers were rooting for her.

Lyle Boyer said, "Good luck, Penny. Show 'em how it can be done."

Penny said, "Thanks. Not yet, Hope. Will you wait a darn second!"

Nine and a half minutes later, Penny came off the course white-faced and silent. Hope had ignored her whistle commands, every shout and entreaty.

NORTH CAROLINA STATE CHAMPIONSHIP

June 14, Bedford, North Carolina
Judge: Ralph Pulfer, Quincy, Ohio

56 Open dogs went to the post

1. Ransome Barlow	Bute	90
2. Kent Kuykendall	Bill	88
3. Roy Brown	Peg	87
4. Roy Johnson	Roscoe	87 (Decided on outwork)
5. Bernie Feldman	Byrn	86

"I DON'T KNOW what I'd do, dog crossed over on his outrun like that," Ransome said.

"I don't recall anybody asking you," Penny said.

June 17, Lexington, Kentucky
Judge: Jack Knox, Butler, Missouri

60 Open dogs went to the post

1. Tom Wilson	Roy	91
2. Barbara Ligon	Jen	89
3. Marilyn Fischer	Chance	87
4. Stu Ligon	Cap	86
5. Karen Thomason	Lad	84

ETHEL HARWOOD SAID "Sometimes young dogs get fed up with all this trialing."

It couldn't have been hotter. Ethel and Penny sat in the shade of Ethel's motor home and drank ice tea.

"That ain't what he's fed up with," Penny said.

"That nice young Texan, Oren what's his name? He went home did he?"

"Wright. Yep."

UNITED STATES BORDER COLLIE CLUB
SHEEPDOG HANDLER'S CLINIC

July 2, 3, 4
White Post, VA
Instructor: Ms. Penny Burkeholder

This year's clinic will be divided into beginning handlers and, on July Fourth, advanced. We will be limited to twenty dogs each day and each dog will be worked twice under Ms. Burkeholder's supervision.

Our Instructor, Ms. Burkeholder, has had a wonderful year on the trial field, placing high in most of the trials she's entered and winning the Blue Ridge Trial and Seclusival. Her father, Lewis Burkeholder, is also quite well known in sheepdog circles.

Food: Every participant will be expected to bring one reheatable main dish, a bread or salad and a dessert. Single men attending may bring enough cold cuts for two meals. We will eat lunch together on Friday, Saturday, and Sunday.

Decorum: All dogs will be chained or leashed when not being worked. No dog will work except under Ms. Burkeholder's permission.

THIS IS A WORKING SHEEP DOG CLINIC. THOSE WHO IMPEDE THE WORK WILL BE ASKED TO LEAVE.

Send your check of $75 (two days, beginner) or $50 (one day advanced) to: Ethel Conrad
Sunnybrook Farm
White Post, VA 22663

Tips and insights poured out of Penny in such an overwhelming flood that some novice handlers quit listening by noon of the first morning. Those who stayed with her noticed she kept returning to one theme: the trust that must exist between handler and dog, how the dog that loses trust is said to be 'soured' and will no longer work.

"Training is like a conversation," she said. "The dog who doesn't trust you won't talk."

JACKPOT SHEEPDOG TRIAL

July 24, Independence, Iowa
Judge: Roy Johnson, Gladys, Virginia

23 Open dogs went to the post

1. Ransome Barlow	Bute	94
2. Penny Burkeholder	Hope	90
3. Dick Bruner	Mac	88
4. Mike Neary	Cap	87
5. George Conboy	Raina	82

BANGOR FAIR OPEN TRIAL

July 31, Bangor Maine
Judge: Walt Jagger, Hop Bottom, Pennsylvania

34 Open dogs went to the post

1. Penny Burkeholder	Hope	96
2. Eve Marschark	Spin	89
3. Dick Williams	Jess	88
4. Mike Canaday	Jill	87
5. Ransome Barlow	Bute	80

"I don't know where that judge got six points off that drive," Ransome said.

"You really expect me to answer that?"

145

MINNESOTA STOCKDOG ASSOCIATION TRIAL

August 8, Taylor, Minnesota
Judge: Bud Boudreau, Marcus, South Dakota

50 Open dogs went to the post

1. Ransome Barlow	Bute	89
2. Penny Burkeholder	Hope	87
3. Chuck O'Reilly	Shep	86
4. Lyle Boyer	Jock	85
5. Florence Wilson	Kate	84

EASTERN ONTARIO TRIPLE CROWN SHEEPDOG TRIAL

August 15–22, Belleville, Stittsville, Kingston, Ontario
Judge: Ralph Pulfer, Quincy, Ohio

70 Open dogs went to the post (Cumulative score)

1. Penny Burkeholder	Hope	576
2. Walt Jagger	Dot	559
3. Pat Buckley	Bart	554
4. Cheryl Jagger Williams	Kim	540
5. Amanda Milliken	Hazel	506

IOWA STATE FAIR STOCKDOG TRIAL

August 29, DesMoines, Iowa
Judge: Mike Neary, Brookston, Iowa

18 Open dogs went to the post

1. Ransome Barlow	Bute	90
2. Penny Burkeholder	Hope	89½
3. Dick Bruner	Mac	88
4. Lewis Pulfer	Creed	86
5. George Conboy	Tammy	85

146

"I HATE these little arena trials. Powerful dog can't get far enough off his sheep. Everything gets speeded up."

"Everybody runs the same course," Ransome said.

"That isn't what I meant."

"I don't know what I'd do, dog pushed his sheep like that," Ransome said.

"Nobody asked you," Penny said.

His head on the transmission hump, Hope panted. It was ninety-five degrees. Waterloo, Burkeville, Center City, Iowa. Flat lands, no windbreaks between the farms, three of four farmhouses abandoned and no motion in the corn rows that dipped and rose as they marched to the horizon. Penny's arm made a *thwock* when she lifted it off the windowsill. Heat mirages danced on the narrow blacktop.

"Look at that," Penny said.

"Somebody's torn out the wall of that farmhouse so he could store his machinery. That's his combine in there."

"God, this is lonely country."

Ransome shrugged. "They went off to the cities where they got good jobs. What's so bad about that?"

"I've already got thirty-one dogs signed up for my clinic."

"Oregon's all right. They got some good dogs out in Oregon. You do many clinics you better get yourself a spare dog. It's hard on a trial dog working clinics."

"Everything's hard on a trial dog."

"Yeah." They whipped past a shabby one-room schoolhouse, half hidden in the weeds. "That's where I went," Ransome said. "My ma's house was a mile down that road. I was in the last class to graduate from that school. God how I hated it. High school was better. They had the shop classes in high school."

They toured tableland above a shallow tree-lined river before swooping down toward the town on its banks. JOHNSON CITY; WELCOME RURITANS!

The houses were white frame, most of them, a few brick ranches. The lawns were well kept and several had sprinklers going. It would have been an attractive town square except for cut-down elm stumps, which let too much light onto the business facades. Courthouse, Woolworth (CLOSED, FOR LEASE), Rexall Drug, several gift and antique shops, one on the ground floor of the stone building that once housed the Johnson City First National Bank. The shedlike building that was the Word of Faith Pentecostal Church might have been a movie theater once. Out on the strip, there wasn't much to see. Oil dealer, Napa Autoparts, closed John Deere dealer: FLEA MARKET EVERY SATURDAY!! Three pickups and two old full-size American cars snugged their noses to Lucille's, a cinderblock bar-restaurant that was windowless but had air conditioners sticking out its side walls, like ears.

The tableland they climbed onto was dry grazing land—sagebrush and jimson weed, gold in the late summer heat.

"This is it," Ransome said, "Home."

A jackrabbit looked up from his nibbling when they pulled off the road. A thousand feet overhead, a vulture watched the jack's passage with mild interest. Broken glass sparkled among the weeds where the gas pumps used to be. At ground level, on the broken concrete, the temperature was 102 degrees. The plywood over the windows and front door was painted the same blue as the cloud-wisped sky, and the lettering across the front was red, faded to ruddy: BARLOW'S MERCANTILE, JOHNSON CITY, IOWA, ELEVATION: 1,395.

When Ransome got out, he kicked an empty two-liter Coke bottle into the sagebrush. "Damn kids."

Penny and Hope got out and stretched. Their shadows were short and afraid to wander from their feet. "Four more hours to Omaha," Penny announced.

"This was a good business once. Sixty thousand dollars gross I had. And the gas tanks were new. No problem with the EPA."

Penny covered her yawn.

Ransome stooped to inspect a shutter where someone had pried at it and bashed the nails back in with a rock. "I got insurance," he said. "Oh yes, I keep up the insurance."

When he jumped Bute out, Bute actually wagged his tail before he dashed around back to his old kennel.

Ransome scuffed the lintel slab clean before he dragged at the steel door. It made an awful noise but came halfway open. "Come in," Ransome invited. "I keep the electric on." When he tapped a switch, four banks of fluorescents popped and sputtered into life. "See anything you want," Ransome said. "Just take it."

The coolers and freezers were empty, but the shelves were stacked with the ordinary merchandise of a country convenience store: cans of baked beans and pinto beans and brown beans and tomatoes and boxes of lasagna mix. There were snack crackers—mice had torn into them—cans of Skoal and Red Man racked beside the silent cash register. The calendar behind the counter supported the Johnson County Sheriff, Jack Froelicher. It was turned to April, four years ago.

Ransome said, "That's how long I been on the road. Saw my first sheepdog trial that fall, tried eight other dogs before I

149

found Bute, and once he was ready I sold the sheep, gave away all the beer and wine and cooler merchandise—eggs, bacon, lunchmeat. I boarded up the place."

Grainy unpainted plywood blocked the big window frames. Dead flies dotted the counter and crunched under Penny's feet. A green brocaded curtain covered the opening behind the counter. PRIVATE, NO ADMISSION.

"I'd like to use your bathroom," Penny said.

"Be my guest."

The bathroom was tiny: shower, sink, commode. A drip plunked into the rusty shower stall, ten thousand plunks a year, wearing through the paint, eventually the steel, eventually the concrete floor. A washcloth hung over the shower rail, stiff, gray and old.

The rest of Ransome's apartment was badly lit. The kitchen stove loomed like a white motherly ghost, the refrigerator was painted some darker color. The living room was carpeted with something that looked like brown AstroTurf, the lounger in front of the TV was black vinyl. Shelves held Ransome's motorcycle trophies and Penny thought she saw some sheepdog trophies too but had no desire to inspect them. She came out of Ransome's private quarters quick, like maybe she'd be trapped if she stayed.

Ransome was out back where empty doghouses faced a small circular training pen. The training pen was grown up with weeds, knee-deep blue-gray weeds Penny'd never seen before. Bute was lying in one of the doghouses, cleaning his paws.

Hope lifted his leg and left his signature across another dog's scent, so faint it was almost memory.

"I am Jack," the old scent whispered. "A good dog."

Behind the corral, high plains stretched on across the continent. "Sixty thousand clear." Ransome scuffed the dirt with his toe. He looked up at Penny. "I don't suppose you're interested."

"It's greener where I come from," Penny said. "Shenandoah Valley gets forty inches rain every year."

"Things have been different since you've been traveling with me," he said. "Hell"—he kicked a pebble against the block well—you were right to take that dog to the vet. Even though it didn't do no good. I don't think I'd like to travel by myself anymore."

Penny raised her eyebrows. "Did I say I was leaving?"

"I don't really care what you did with that Oren fellow. You're free, white, and twenty-one."

"Twenty-six."

"I mean, hell. I suppose you think this place is pretty ugly. Well, it isn't anything to me. We find a place somewhere else, I can sell this."

"Ransome, I know you are a fine dog handler and I owe you for teaching me. You've been a good friend. I don't think I could have tolerated a better one. So far as I'm concerned, we can keep on traveling together. But that's that."

Ransome jammed his hat down on his head and called Bute. "Get in the truck. We're burning daylight."

The buzzard hung there as the pickup screeched back onto the road and sped away. The buzzard hoped that jackrabbit might choose that precise moment to cross the blacktop, but the bunny stayed at the roadside and wriggled his ears.

◌

September 1, Beaver Creek, Oregon
Judge: Dodie Green, Buckeye, Arizona

20 Open dogs went to the post

1. Ransome Barlow	Bute	88
2. Penny Burkeholder	Hope	86
3. Donald Boyd	Nell	86 (Decided on outwork)
4. Pat Shannahan	Hannah	84
5. Candy Kennedy	Sage	82

NOP NEVER HAD any particular regrets about growing old, never wished his life might have been different. In his bed, he dreamed of himself as he'd been, sweeping easily around great flocks, light on his feet—for a few moments when he woke, gray muzzled and old, he was disoriented—but soon he was back in his own skin again, leaving his dream skin for tomorrow night.

One morning, a month ago, Lewis took Nop out to the sheep. They made dark paths through dewy grass, Nop dashing from side to side. It was cool on the riverbank and Lewis paused under the big maple where he and his Daddy had rested their hay horses in the old days. "I dunno, Nop," he said. "I suppose it's worth a try."

Nop wagged his tail. He looked at the sheep, two hundred yards away.

"Just a couple old fools, you and me, trying to make a comeback. We were a team once, you remember, Nop?"

Nop wished Lewis would quit talking. The sheep were drifting over a low rise and some were already out of sight.

"You think we can win again? Has-beens like us?"

Nop wagged his tail, game for anything.

"Well then," Lewis said, "away to me!" And Nop was off.

If dog trialing was all Penny Burkeholder admired, her father could do that too. He and Nop would lay down such a run on the trial field, his daughter would be restored to him.

Nop had no inkling why Lewis wanted to trial again. He loved the work, the training, taking seriously what had become mere routine. Nop had slowed, but he made up for that by sheepdog wisdom. Over his life, he had herded thousands of different sheep: old ones, sprightly ones, defiant rams, sick old ewes, goofy lambs, and the mothers who'd die to protect them.

As Lewis worked with his old pal, he found new ways to trust him, found times where the old dog could manage sheep the young Nop couldn't have.

The first trial they ran was the Virginia State Fair Trial in Richmond. A small arena, with a hundred yard outrun, it should have been a piece of cake, but Nop couldn't get far enough off his sheep, Lewis lost his cool, and they were lucky to finish third.

Nop enjoyed himself (more, perhaps, than Lewis did), and on the drive home, he rode right on the front seat with his head on Lewis's leg, so deeply asleep the oncoming headlights that splashed the pickup didn't bother him at all and he drooled a bit and he snored.

153

When Lewis came into the kitchen, Beverly looked up from her magazine. "There's a beef stew on the warming oven."

Nop went to his bed behind the wood stove and pawed himself a nest and grunted once after he lay down: sufficient unto the day. Lewis looked at his wife, and thought how lucky he was to have married well, how most of the good things in his life had flowed from that. He bent and gave her a kiss on the top of the head.

"What's that for?" she asked.

"Oh, nothing. That stew smells good."

Lewis trained his dog and Beverly taught Sunday school and passed out donated canned goods at the church food pantry, each making prayers—that their daughter might be restored to them. They were parents and merely human.

Ransome Barlow was too linear for prayer. As a hard-shelled midwestern pragmatist, he played the cards he was dealt. His case ace, as he saw it, was dog handling. That Texas fellow, Oren What's-his-name, couldn't touch him there. He didn't like that Penny had gone off with What's-his-name at Oatlands, but there was no helping it. Maybe he should have been sweeter to Penny early on, but there was no helping that either.

Maybe he'd got too set in his ways. Penny had opened doors in his life that he'd never known were there. He didn't know about getting married and all that, but he surely didn't want to lose her.

Until they started riding together, she'd had a rough time of it. Who was that cowman who knew those rapists but wouldn't give them up? Ransome Barlow knew he couldn't offer Penny Burkeholder stability, children, community approval, money in the bank—none of those things. But he could keep her safe.

LIKE MOST COUNTY FAIR TRIALS, the course was in a horse arena, and since the trial was held at night, the Ferris wheel and the dipper and whirligig were turning and blaring rock music, made it hard to think. Up went the wheel of lights, climbing the stars, around looped the whirligig, lurch and stop swooped the hammer.

The announcer said, "FROM FAR OFF VIRGINNY, MS. PENNY BURKEHOLDER AND HOPE. THIS DUO BEEN WINNIN' SOME BIG TRIALS LATELY, FOLKS. WASN'T THAT FINE!"

Ransome motioned to Penny when she came off the course.

"Don't tie your dog to the truck. I'm going away for a couple weeks. I've got some business which you ain't no part of. I already talked to Miz Harwood. She got all your stuff. You can travel with her out to Fort Collins."

"Hey," Penny said, "it's my truck too."

He said, "I'll buy you out."

She said, "What if I don't want to sell?"

He pocketed his wallet. "That's fine then. I'll meet you in Colorado."

Ethel touched Penny's arm. "It'll be fine, Penny. We'll have a great time."

"Goddamnit, that's not the point!" Penny said. But the next minute Barlow was gone.

. . .

OKLAHOMA CATTLEMAN'S ASSOCIATION didn't answer their phone. Oklahoma Department of Agriculture said Ransome could leave a message at the tone. Oklahoma State Fair said he should wait for an operator, and Ransome fed quarters into the pay phone while the recorded message listed events at the upcoming State Fair. Finally, an operator.

"One of your exhibitors is Jack Dickerson. I'm looking to buy a bull from him and need his phone number."

"Oh, no sir, we're not allowed to give that out."

"Uh-huh. Well I'm headin' south tomorrow. What town's he in?"

"I suppose it's all right to tell you that. That's printed on the premium list."

Dickerson Land and Cattle's secretary said, sorry, Mr. Dickerson wasn't available. If Mr. Jones could leave his phone number, Mr. Dickerson would get back to him soon as he got back from Denver.

By five o'clock the next morning, Ransome Barlow was in Denver. The livestock gate behind the colosseum was wide open, and Ransome parked his pickup in the shade of a tremendous cattle truck. The sun was just streaking the sky, orange and purple as cowboys led show cattle softly along, clucking to the two-ton beasts that followed at their heels, docile as mice. A jet from Denver's Stapleton Airport lifted into the sky, and the sun washed its wings silver.

The colosseum was a cavernous place, and without the golden straw in the pens and the meat density of all those cattle the place would have echoed.

Simmentals, Chianinas, Limousin, Angus, Brangus, and Hereford: the cows looked up as Ransome passed and one or two mooed. It was breakfast time.

Dickerson Land and Cattle's big pens straddled the intersection of the main aisles. One pen was reserved for tack, harness halters, a stack of rubber buckets. Another held the Dickerson cattle display. Photographs of people gripping the halters of award-winning cows and bulls and a video screen, presently blank, and a pamphlet box, presently empty, which suggested that Ransome should: READ HOW CALF PROFITS CAN SOAR.

A skinny young cowgirl under a terrific white western hat was mucking out a pen into a wheelbarrow.

No, Mr. Dickerson ain't here. He generally didn't come by until noon. They'd be showing the two-year-old cows then.

"Thank you, ma'am."

The sun washed the sunrise out of the sky, the jet trails got white and ordinary, a twittering flight of swallows scooped morning insects out of the air.

Ransome fed and watered Bute and settled himself into the show grandstand, first row where he could put his feet up on the rail, and daydreamed. The cattle show was 4-H Limousin heifers, calves born before January first. Family members filled the stands as youngsters led their animals into the ring. The kids wore identical white coveralls, spotless, and their parents coached them urgently from the sidelines. "He's watchin' you, honey, the judge! Look sharp!"

The crowd had thickened, the western wear shop was open for business, cattle chute and gate manufacturers were promoting their wares. At the hat store Ransome tried on a Resistol 5x hat but didn't buy. He'd get another year out of his old hat. He leaned against a steel stanchion, just another cowboy in a colosseum full of cowboys.

Jack Dickerson arrived with an entourage, but there was no mistaking who was the Boss. Dickerson was the fellow with whipcords tucked into the new Tony Lamas, the fellow with the 15x El Patron Stetson with the ruby-studded hat band. Dickerson was the fellow doing all the talking and his two cowboys, foreman, and the little girl Ransome had met earlier scurried hither and yon at his bidding. The foreman brought out a big steer, and one of the cowboys took it to the washrack. Another cowboy plugged in the video machine so it could start its hymns of praise to Dickerson stock.

Ransome hung back until Dickerson was looking around for the next thing to do. Then he started his pitch, waving his pickup registration. "Mr. Dickerson, Ransome Barlow, here's the papers on that truck."

Up close Dickerson's eyes were red veined and his cologne barely outstank the whiskey he'd drunk last night.

"What papers you talkin' about, son?"

"For that pickup Marvin bought. Now if you'll just sign a receipt, I can be on my way."

"Whoa, hold up a minute. Don't get your butt in an uproar, son. What pickup, what papers?"

"Marvin bought this truck out in Santa Fe, and he hired me to bring it to Denver, said I could deliver it to you and you'd sign for it. It's a real cattle show, ain't it? We got some shows in New Mexico, but I never seen nothin' like these. These Chianinas, I tell you, they are real cows. We used to use them Chianina calves for roping, you know, but we quit. Too many times some cowboy came down his rope and the calf was coming back at him, ha, ha. Well it's nice meeting you, truck's out in aisle D, blue Dodge."

This was all Jack Dickerson needed, a hangover and all this noise coming at him and some craziness about a pickup that wasn't his, and he didn't want to have anything to do with it. He pushed the papers back at Ransome. "Marvin ain't here."

"Well," Ransome backed away, "I wouldn't know about that, would I? He said bring the pickup here and you'd take care of it. I already bought my bus ticket home." He patted his pocket. "Maybe one of your hands give me a ride down to the Greyhound?"

Dickerson dropped the registration papers, but Ransome was at them, had them gathered up, was thrusting them at Dickerson again. "I ain't gonna be responsible for another man's pickup."

The foreman stepped closer and said, "Mr. Dickerson, I think you should take a look at 477, something wrong with her jaw."

"It's Marvin's pickup and I'm supposed to deliver it here and I done delivered it."

"Marvin's in Twin Bridges, he ain't here."

Very much later that day, ensconced in a leather chair, sipping his second Jack Daniel's in the colosseum's Silver Spur Club, Jack Dickerson brought his mind back to that cowboy and his pickup. A rancher from Spanish Fork, Utah, squeezed his shoulder. "That was a hell of a yearling bull, Jack. Fine-looking animal."

"Thanks Jim. That hard-headed judge, he finally saw it our way." What had that cowboy been yammering about?

When the light dawned, a slow grin crossed Jack Dickerson's face. Wasn't that often he was had. It crossed his mind to warn Marvin, but he got to talking cows with a couple fellows and what with one thing and another . . .

Enroute to Twin Bridges, Montana, Ransome stopped

twice for gas, bought a ham and cheese sandwich from a machine and in the True Value hardware store in Moroni, Idaho, he bought an axe handle, two pounds, kiln dried hickory, twenty-eight inches long.

RANSOME PARKED in the Kiwanis International picnic ground, beside the Madison River. The mountains in the distance were clear and indifferent and purple. No telling how far away. The riverbank grass was taller than his knees, and a path wandered to a sandbar and Ransome supposed fishermen made it. Four neat picnic tables had been painted dark green over old initials. Somewhere out in the reeds a meadow lark gurgled. Ransome snatched a mosquito out of the air, but when he opened his palm it escaped.

Somewhere a dog barked but Bute didn't hardly look up as he drank his fill from the clear stream. A car passed by on Highway 10. Ransome got another mosquito and rubbed him dead against his pant leg. He put Bute back in his crate.

In a cafe on Main Street, he was too late for the dinner special: country steak with home fries and green beans, so he had a couple ham sandwiches, mayo on white, and tore a bag of potato chips off the rack. The waitress was telling the cook about her boyfriend, who'd gone to be a miner in Butte. The cook was a bony fellow, no hips: his belt wrapped around twice. Ransome left two quarters for a tip and at the cash register, asked, "Where's a man go if he's looking for a good time?" He drank maybe one beer a year, usually when somebody handed it to him. He had no use for drunks. If he wanted an animal he'd take Bute. At least Bute kept himself clean. "Honky-tonk," he added.

"They got beer at Marsha's Hideaway, outside of town, Highway 10," the cook said slowly.

"Or?"

"The Bar None. On the flats behind the stockyards. It can get rough."

Ransome rolled a toothpick out of the plastic machine and nodded his thanks and the waitress locked the door behind him.

In his camper, Ransome unrolled his foam mattress and sleeping bag. He had planned to sleep for an hour but didn't wake until midnight. The moon was full as he hunkered down beside the river to splash water on his face.

Excited cars howled by, followed by a shout, tires complained and a motor wound through the gears: any western town on Saturday night.

On Main Street a handful of Indians leaned against a pickup. They didn't wave.

Bar O
BEER & SPIRITS

A dirt road dipped behind the stockyards. Whatever animals were inside were asleep and the moon painted the board fences dirty white.

Ransome rattled across a one-lane bridge into the parking lot. Somebody wearing a Texas hat came outdoors, disappeared behind a pickup and took a long noisy whizz. The flare of a match lit his cigarette as Ransome stepped out of the darkness. "Marvin inside?"

"Where the hell else would he be?" The cowboy flipped his match and sucked his smoke to a glow.

An oversized moon outshone the stars. A nighthawk swooped over the stream harvesting mosquitoes.

The Bar None was one long room with a bandstand (unoccupied and dark) at the one end, signs: POINTER, SETTER over doors at the other. The jukebox played Charley Pride pretty loud and flashed its neon glitter. Elk heads and four scruffy mule deer ornamented the back bar above an electric waterfall: OLYMPIA, IT'S THE WATER. The bartender was a blond-haired fellow with a headache pinch in his forehead.

"Draft," Ransome announced and idly surveying the room he added, "bring a drink to Marvin."

The bartender gave him a look but flagged a waitress in a shabby cowgirl outfit, poured a double whiskey, which she carried to a back table walled with beer cans. Three cowboys: brown hat, white hat, straw hat. Brown hat looked up surprised, raised his arm in thanks.

Ransome sipped his beer; beer hadn't changed since last he drank it.

"Do I know you?" Voice at his elbow, sweat, whiskey, after-shave.

Ransome stuck out his paw, "Mack Sorenson's my name, Waco, Texas. Friend of Jack Dickerson."

"Old Jack—*muy hombre,* that one. Christ, if I had that man's balls. Who'd you say your name was?"

"Sorenson. Know anybody up here lookin' for a stockman? Cows, sheep, okay with me. No hogs though. I hate their damn stink."

"Waco, Texas—Christ, I wish I was back in Texas. Montana ain't been nothin' but trouble to me. Come on over, meet the boys."

Two men sat backs to the wall, determined not to repeat Wild Bill Hickok's mistake. The younger man was taller, darker complected, but even a stranger could see the family resemblance.

"P.T. McVey here's just about the best calf roper there is," Marvin made introductions, "and this here's his boy, Bobby. Bobby's a stick-in-the-mud." Though he paused, he got no response from the younger man. "Chrissakes. Can't you take a joke?"

Ransome dragged over a chair and straddled it.

"Hell," Marvin said, for no particular reason. "Hell." Then he added, "Mack's from Waco, Texas."

"Jack Dickerson said to give you his best. He was working the Fort Worth show with you last January."

"Was we in Texas in January?" Marvin's face tried to work out the answer. "Christ my memory's shot." He laughed, "You see here a good man wrecked by whiskey and drugs. Bobby, why don't you be a good fellow and go up to the bar and get us a round? I don't think they're gonna serve me no more."

Bobby McVey was probably eighteen. His hair was slicked back, his shirt fresh pressed, his blue jeans pressed. Wordlessly, he paused at Ransome's elbow, "Somethin' for you?"

"I still got this one," Ransome said, sliding it around on the tabletop.

"Bobby don't approve of the company his Daddy keeps," Marvin giggled. "Hell, I don't approve of the company his Daddy keeps." He tilted his glass to his mouth and tried to find something in it.

"Thanks, good buddy," P.T. muttered. His chin slipped off his hand but he caught it just in time. "First day we met, Ol' Marvin was pushin' steers around the old Cheyenne stock-market. They closed that down didn't they? The old west is goin', son. I'll be glad to be dead before it goes."

"Last of the short loop boys." The young man set a tray on the table: beers for P.T. and Marvin, a Dr Pepper for himself. "That'll be four dollars," he said and waited as Marvin pulled four faded singles out of his wallet. Bobby popped the tab on his can of soda. "What brings you here, Waco, Texas? Things too hot down by the Rio Grande?"

Ransome sipped his beer, rolled it around in his mouth. How could people drink this stuff? "Might be," he drawled.

Marvin barked a laugh. "You asked him, boy. You asked!"

Some cowboy shoved two bits into the jukebox and Tanya Tucker wailed into action and the bartender put down the glass he'd been polishing and dipped his hand below the bar and the jukebox fell to a whisper.

Bobby turned to Ransome. "I'm the baby-sitter. They're in so much trouble if they get in any more, they're purely gonna drown."

P.T. protested, "I told that fool lawyer he should put me on the stand. Wasn't nobody owned those calves, wasn't no brand on a one of them. They was from that old Bohunk's herd, down by the Big Hole, and he pulled up stakes three years ago, just up and left them. They was mavericks, and we had as much right to those calves as any man. I would have testified, but Mr. Smart Lawyer, no, oh no."

"If them steers hadn't been locked up in the Ferris Brothers' corral and if you hadn't shot the padlock off and if you'd took 'em in the daylight, maybe you could have been on the stand."

Marvin wrinkled his mouth. "God, I hate a smartmouth kid."

P.T. laughed. "I would have like to see those Ferris Brothers that morning when they show up with their crew, do a little brandin' and no calves anywhere. 'Here Calvey, Calvey? Here, Calf? Now, where *are* those blame things?' "

"Yeah," Bobby said. "Everybody's laughing and you're going to Deer Lodge Prison."

Marvin said, "Got to be better'n Huntsville. I'll take Deer Lodge if it comes to it and just hope it satisfies Texas."

Bobby yawned. "You 'bout drunk enough?"

"Oh Christ, I dunno," P.T. said. "You drunk enough, Marvin? Seems to me I could get more drunk if I had a mind to."

"Boy wants to go home," Marvin said. "Might be he has homework to do."

Ransome leaned forward. "Jack Dickerson said you two were Real People. Said you'd do to ride the river with. You crappin' out on me?"

"Thanks a lot, Mister," Bobby said.

Marvin grinned. "Hell, why don't we get a bottle and drive out to the Bitterroot. Morning, we'll catch some cutthroat trout, make a fire, eat 'em on the spot. Don't that sound fine."

"We could go into Butte. Find the boy a whore, get him blooded."

The boy's ear got red.

"I don't know if I got enough left for a bottle." Marvin looked pointedly at Ransome.

"Any special brand?" Ransome stood.

"Nothin' wrong with Four Roses."

When Ransome paid, the bartender leaned over his bar. "Mister, if I was you, I'd be careful around those two."

"They don't look dangerous to me."

"There's fellas love to see them step over the line right now. And them fellas drive cars with light bars on the roof."

When he stepped into the darkness outside the Bar None, Ransome's pupils contracted so quickly they hurt.

"Christ, I got to pee." Marvin stumbled off, unzipping himself.

"What do you want?" the boy asked Ransome.

Ransome shrugged. "Job, woman, little fun. What does any man want?"

"Here. Now."

Ransome pasted a false smile on his face. "Son, it's Saturday night and I just got paid."

The boy's pickup was a ten-year-old red Ford, with a homemade paint job that continued over the hood emblem. "We could take my truck," Ransome said.

Marvin opened his mouth but the boy was shaking his head, "No. I got plenty of gas."

"Damn, I miss my F250, 348 cubic inches, interceptor tires, come down the road in that truck, they knew I was comin'."

"You was lucky you had it to sell," the boy said, dryly. "That truck bought you a second-rate lawyer."

"Tell me again, son. Why is it you won't let me borrow this Ford?"

"Because I'll call the sheriff if you do. Because this truck is about all I got to show. And you know I'll do it."

P.T. turned to Ransome. "This here boy, Mr. Sorenson, is what my life has come to. He's my eldest. Blood of my blood. Ain't it a cryin' shame?"

"Wait a sec," Ransome walked to his truck and got the axe handle and dropped it in the pickup bed.

"What's that for?" Marvin asked.

"I thought we were gonna catch a trout and eat it. We'll need a fire."

"Yeah, but that axe ain't no use. Got no head on it."

"Well then, hell. It'll make firewood."

Marvin laughed and smacked him on the back and said, "You're a real thinker, ain't you, Mack!"

The same Indians attended the same pickup on Twin Bridges's main street and P.T. rapped the horn. The Indians looked up but didn't wave or anything.

"Set the bottle on the floor!" Marvin hissed. "Smokies!"

"I ain't uncorked it," Ransome drawled. "No sweat."

When Bobby stopped at Twin Bridges's single traffic light, the sheriff's deputy pulled up alongside and leaned to see who was driving. Bobby's hands clamped white on the wheel and he stared straight ahead. "Bastards," he muttered.

Didn't keep his father from sticking a hand out the window and giving the deputy a floppy wristed wave.

"They won't pull Bobby over," P.T. explained. "They know he don't drink. He's a teetotaler."

The deputy passed the red truck and disappeared.

Bobby turned into a convenience store on the outskirts of town. "Anybody want a soda? I thought not."

Ransome stretched and came around to the driver's side and got in. Bobby was standing at the counter jawing with a woman clerk, who wasn't much older than he was.

Ransome started the truck and backed away—the boy's astonished face as the headlights swept the store's plate glass.

"Oh Christ," Marvin said. "That's torn it."

"Kid's a little old lady," Ransome said, taking the road straight out of town.

"What if we're stopped?"

"No sweat. I'm sober." Ransome passed the bottle. "You get started on this. Tonight, we are going to have ourselves a Big Time."

"Oh man," P.T. said. "Bobby ain't gonna like this one little bit."

"What's he going to do about it?"

"He said he'd call the cops."

"Drop the dime on his own daddy? Sure he will. Will you look at that moon?"

The road wound along and over the hills, like a black ribbon under the western sky. Big moon, the mountains like sawteeth. They dipped and rose onto a mesa where all the world lay open to them.

Ransome pulled off into a highway department gravel pit and cut the lights. "Screw Bobby," he said.

"Oh, man," P.T. said. "When that boy was born I was so proud, I thought I'd just bust. His mama was a Calhoun girl, only child that mossback ever had, and I figured I was set for life. Young wife and new son and granddad owned four thousand deeded acres and an eighteen-thousand acre BLM allotment. Where's that bottle, Marvin?"

"First, our host," Marvin said, with tipsy elegance.

When Ransome lifted the bottle, he plugged the opening with his tongue and drank nothing at all. "Good stuff," he pronounced.

"I had it made in the shade, partner. Made in the shade. So what'd I do? Start looking around and what do I find but this girl cheerleader. She's got braces and she ain't got no tits to speak of and she don't know more about making love than a knothole in a fence, but I got to have her. Braces, I swear to Christ. I start dragging the wife and the kid and granddaddy to all the high school football games. Granddad knows I played ball myself, but he didn't have any idea what I'm coming to see: Connie, Connie Malloy. Here's to you, Connie. You'd think Connie would have been satisfied. I was good lookin', had money, my own 4 x 4, but that two-timing tramp was making it with half the damn backfield, and me so love struck, sooner or later I was bound to get caught. I thought my wife would understand, would give me a chance to explain. All I wanted"—P.T. laughed—"was a chance to tell a few good lies. That's all any man wants. Gimme that Four Roses."

A semi steamed by. Ransome blinked away from the headlight brightness. Marvin lit a cigarette and Ransome opened the door and leaned against the cab, one foot on the running board. The axe handle gleamed in the moonlight, inches from his hand.

"You were in Texas in January," Ransome said quietly.

"At the Fat Stock show, you bet."

The axe handle felt slick and cool under Ransome's palm. "Remember the girl?" Ransome asked.

"Here, your turn," Marvin pushed the bottle at him.

Ransome said, "Why not get out of the truck."

"Sure thing, partner," P.T. said, but when he opened the door he hung on it, half swung. "Whoops" he said, "don't fly so good as I usta."

"The girl with the dog, remember her?"

P.T. hung on the door, head down, and laughing. "Oh hell, I done forgot all about that girl. Remember, Marvin? I swore you like to change your shorts on that one. That dog come through that window like King Kong. Ol' Marvin, he was gettin' himself ready to boogie before Mr. Dog showed up."

"It weren't funny at the time," Marvin said.

"Why don't you get out of the truck," Ransome said quietly.

"Why? I seen moonlight and I seen a gravel pit and I even seen you before." Marvin fumbled at the dash until he found the radio. It was a rap group singing and their syncopation seemed alien under the big western night.

Ransome reached in to shut it off. "Man," he said, "you are one ugly bastard."

Marvin's face sobered. "Who you, partner? Some friend of Jack Dickerson? Get me in trouble with P.T.'s kid? You come from Texas to tell me I'm ugly? You think I don't know that? Listen." He punched the radio on and it resumed its blare, a howling puny mockery of all those distant blue mountains, all those diamond stars. He hollered, "Some of us, partner, are born to be ugly." He laughed. "P.T.?"

P.T. swung out, swung back. "Yeah, Marvin."

"You remember that girl, Texas, the one with the dog?"

"Should have shot that dog," P.T. said dreamily.

"Dog was beautiful, P.T."

Suddenly Marvin jerked his door shut and pushed the button and rolled the window up. "P.T., get inside," he yelled.

"Who? Oh what you doing, Marvin? What you doing now?"

Marvin grabbed P.T. by the back of the collar and dragged him into the cab and P.T. was sober enough to fight but too drunk to know who to fight so he smacked the nearest man, who happened to be Marvin, slammed his elbow into Marvin's gut.

"You son of a bitch," Marvin gasped and grapped P.T.'s ears and rolled him between the seat and the dashboard. He pounded his partner on top of the head.

P.T. was flailing away, both men were grunting and panting and Ransome stood immobile, his axe handle forgotten.

The moon shimmered in the truck's polished hood as it rocked from side to side. Absently, Ransome turned and hurled his axe handle at the sky. It luminesced as it flipped over before it dropped into the shadows behind the gravel pit.

It was easy walking on the highway. Frogs chirped from the irrigation ditches and a sleepy meadow lark twittered an inquiry from the unmown verge. It was quiet back in the gravel pit, no more curses or blows.

The truck door slammed, a bottle crashed. The motor caught on the last crank of the battery and the driver gunned the engine. Ransome kept up his steady stride.

When the truck came onto the highway, the headlights wobbled all over the place.

Ransome walked out into the sagebrush before the truck got near enough to see him and knelt until the drunken truck was safely by.

That road was his alone in that moonlight and it would have been a fine time to think about the meaning of life if he'd been of a mind to.

Twin Bridges was a cluster of lights. Sodium lights guarded garages, silent businesses, and defined the convenience store where they'd left young Bobby.

Bobby's red Ford was skewed across the shoulder where the cops had forced it off. Except for their smell, Marvin and P.T. were long gone. The driver's door hung open and the headlight filaments still glowed their faint yellow glow. Ransome cut the lights and closed the door. That boy never did any harm.

September 1, Monterey, Virginia
Judge: Tom Forrester, Aldie, Virginia

22 Open dogs went to the post

1. Lewis Burkeholder	Nop	91
2. Ethel Conrad	Jan	88
3. Ed Gebauer	Flo	87
4. Kay Pine	Molly	84
5. Roy Johnson	June	83

LEWIS BURKEHOLDER took his blue ribbon from the judge's hand and shook hands and said, yes, Nop had run well for an older dog. He clipped the ribbon to his shirt pocket while a couple of kids got their fill of petting Nop. Beverly was talking to her cousins. Beverly's mother had come from Highland County, and in years past this little trial was the only one Beverly attended, catching up with her kinfolk while the dogs ran.

The cousins, both in their sixties, marveled at the Burkeholders' RV, said, "Isn't it homey," and "It's just like a ship inside." They congratulated Lewis and petted Nop and said, "I'll bet that dog saves you some steps."

173

Lewis said yes indeed, indeed he did and asked Beverly if she wanted to see the rest of the fair.

The cousins said, "Don't let us keep you," and "Beverly, honey, we'll just have to get together real soon," and "We were so upset to hear about your granddaughter. Mary wanted to come up to the funeral but I don't see well at night and Mary doesn't drive."

"It'll be one year the twenty-seventh of this month," Beverly said. "It seems like yesterday."

Beverly held Lewis's arm as they strolled past the stock barns where the 4-H kids were grooming their animals. "Lisa would have been old enough for 4-H this year," Beverly said.

"Uh-huh. Look at that little fellow over there with that steer. I'm not sure who's leading who."

It was afternoon and three roughnecks were repairing the mechanism of the merry-go-round. The candy corn and cotton candy booths had their shutters down, the ring toss booth was closed tight. Two elderly men worked the Ruritan burger booth, one taking orders, the other at the grill. Lewis asked Beverly would she like something and she shook her head. Lewis ordered a cheeseburger and coffee for himself.

Beverly said, "Lewis, you might as well tell me what's on your mind."

"We're going out to Wyoming for the National Finals," Lewis said.

"You might be going," Beverly replied, calmly, "but I have responsibilities. Since January Penny hasn't bothered to call. Postcards: 'won this trial,' 'Hope ran well today.' My only daughter can't talk about anything but her dog. You know how many times a day I think I hear the telephone ring? You go out to do chores, drive to town, I stay right near that blamed old telephone, oh, Lewis . . ."

The Ruritan cook set Lewis's cheeseburger on a square of wax paper beside the coffee, coughed politely, rearranged the catsup and mayonnaise and withdrew.

"I thought we could go out to Wyoming, Beverly, and be with Penny. She might be the national champion, think of that!"

"I don't want any national champion," Beverly said and didn't burst into tears. "I just want my daughter back."

"Maybe Penny'll come on home with us for Thanksgiving and Christmas. I already talked to Joe Maxwell. That road job he was working got finished, so he's laid off. He'll feed and keep an eye on the place. Preacher Shumway, I telephoned him. He thought it was a good idea you going with me, that Penny'd sure want us there supporting her. He said Miz Collins would take your Sunday school class and he'll look in on your mother while we're away."

Beverly looked him straight in the eye, started to say something harsh but said, "You're awfully sure of yourself, aren't you?"

"No," he said, "I'm not at all sure. I think there's a fair chance we'll go out there and make godallmighty fools of ourselves. But I'll feel worse if we lay around the farm like nothing's wrong except we don't talk much about anything important ever and our daughter never writes us or calls us on the telephone. I'd rather go out there even if we fail. I need you with me, Beverly.

"Well then," she said, flustered. "Well then. Imagine that, Lewis. Arizona and Wyoming in one year. You and me are getting to be quite the travelers. You know, when Mamma and Daddy had their honeymoon, they took the train to Philadelphia and that was as far as they traveled the whole of their married life.''

At home, with just a week before they were to leave, Beverly took up her potatoes from the garden and told neighbors they could pick the late peaches because they'd be past when the Burkeholders came home. Beverly took to watching TV weather, morning and evening, to see what the temperatures were in Wyoming, and when snow symbols drifted down from Canada she packed sweaters and Lewis's wooly hat and gloves. She told Lewis there was no reason on earth they should eat poorly away from home and filled the big drawer under the motor home bed with canned tomatoes, canned beans, applesauce, and three jars of pickalilly. She said it was a shame the motor home didn't have a freezer so she could bring along their own meat, some hamburger and a roast or two. Lewis said that the motor home designers certainly missed a trick, that probably lots of people would like to drive across the country eating out of their own freezer.

They got a predawn start and took the northern route, through Iowa and South Dakota. On the second day Beverly said, "Lewis it's like driving a big truck from the comfort of your own living room."

They arrived at Buffalo, Wyoming, Friday afternoon and drove straight out to the trial grounds. They hadn't said a word about Penny all morning.

—————————————— ❧ ——————————————

September 5 & 6, Fort Collins, Colorado
Judge: Jack Knox, Butler, Missouri

48 Open dogs went to the post		1st day	2nd day	Cumulative
1. Penny Burkeholder	Hope	89	91	180
2. Dorrance Eikamp	Blue	90	88	178
3. Pat Shannahan	Hannah	85	85	170
4. Roger Culbreath	Trim	90	79	179
5. Dodie Green	Soot	92	76	168
48. Ransome Barlow	Bute	68	DQ (Grip)	68

MEEKER INTERNATIONAL SHEEPDOG TRIAL
September 12, 13, Meeker, Colorado
Judge: Bill Berhow, Lavina, Montana

70 Open dogs went to the post		1st	2nd day	Cumulative
1. Herbert Holmes	Dave	92	92	184
2. Penny Burkeholder	Hope	90	90	180
3. Bud Boudreau	Patches	84	90	174
4. Don Boyd	Nell	90	81	171
5. Ralph Pulfer	Ken	88	80	168

THE WINNEBAGOS and Pace Arrows and Cherokees and Chieftains and Dodge Astrostars and Wayfarers trundled over the Rocky Mountain passes, sticking close together because the last thing you want is a breakdown in snow country, you and your four dogs.

It was the tail end of the season that had started last January and everyone was showing the wear. One woman handler made a few calculations and announced that if she hadn't wasted her money on sheepdog trials, she could be making payments on a pretty good car, perhaps a Subaru. That set other handlers to pen and pencil. One California handler said, "Subaru hell, I'm good for a Mercedes."

Handlers who'd had a good year were looking forward to the National Finals to put a cap on it. Handlers who hadn't done so well worried openly how things were going back home, complained about feeling stretched between two places they needed to be.

The dogs liked the cooler weather. Every week they were whisked off to a new trial where they'd meet fresh sheep, and fresh countryside and fresh difficulties. Like touring concert musicians all they cared about were their brief, ecstatic performances.

Some of the dogs were too old for the demands, and between trials, they lay in their kennels and dreamed old dog dreams. But when they stepped onto the trial field, miraculously, their gimps and stiffness would evaporate and, exchanging glances with their handler (who was maybe going gray himself), they'd be the powerful young dog who'd set the world afire once upon a time. And handlers would look up from their programs, forget their conversations and come to admire a great dog they'd seen so many times and wouldn't be seeing much longer.

Penny Burkeholder's Hope nipped a sheep at the Meeker

trial but the judge didn't call it. Either the judge was daydream-ing or he was so bemused by the dog's brilliant performance, the nip became a nonevent in his mind.

Of course some handlers bitched about that undetected nip, said, "Some people could do no wrong." Ransome Barlow told anyone who'd listen that "Two years is too damn young for so much heavy trialing," and Ethel Harwood snapped, "He's old enough to beat your dog! Only difference between Hope's nip and Bute's is Bute got caught at it."

Bute hadn't been running at all well. Some people thought the dog had soured, others thought Ransome was handling him badly. Ransome's new pals were the most critical.

"Ransome ain't been right since he came back from Mon-tana," one said. "Goin' away like that broke his string."

Another pal said, "More likely his love life went bad. That Burkeholder gal isn't giving ol' Ransome the time of day."

The first pal said, "Man gets used to it, can't get along without it."

Since neither Ransome nor Penny talked about their breech, other handlers took up the slack. Penny had bought her own pickup, a low-mileage Nissan with a camper. And she wanted her money out of the pickup she and Ransome had shared—everybody knew that. And one of Ransome's new-found pals had been hanging around when Ransome came back when Penny lit into him before he had a chance to explain—he didn't say word one. "That Ransome is too proud to beg," the pal noted approvingly.

Ransome's silent unhappiness attracted new friends—friends who generally popped their first beer before lunch. Al-though these men never finished in the money themselves, they were invariably sympathetic when Ransome had a bad run. "Hell," they'd say, "that damn judge shouldn't have called you off. When *I* beat you, you know something's wrong."

Bute hated these men and somebody would have been dog bit if Ransome hadn't kept Bute locked up.

After Meeker, Nathan Mooney and Herbert Holmes from the Handlers' Association detoured to Sheridan, to check on preparations for the Finals. They worried that the sheep wouldn't arrive, that the cowboys who'd promised to put them out wouldn't show, that the judge would get ill on all this unfamiliar cuisine. (Could buffalo burgers ruin the intestinal flora of a Scottish Highlander?) They worried that the local radio stations and newspapers hadn't given the event enough promotion. They looked up at the Bighorns towering behind the enormous flat course and Herbert asked the trial director, "How early does it snow in these parts?"

"We've seen snow here on Labor Day."

"If it does snow, the dogs can still work but you won't pull much of a crowd."

"The ten-day forecast doesn't say anything about snow."

Herbert rubbed his hands. "It was pretty cold when we came through the pass."

The Bighorns were blue and green in the twilight. The irrigation pipes that watered the Sheridan Equestrian Center throbbed and hissed from all the water thundering through them.

"Well," Herbert said, and shook the trial director's hand, "let's hope. See you in two weeks."

THE BUFFALO PURINA DOG TRIAL

September 19, 20, Buffalo Wyoming
Judge: Bud Boudreau, Marcus, South Dakota

72 Open dogs went to the post

		1st day	2nd day	Cumulative
1. Ransome Barlow	Bute	92	91	183
2. Ralph Pulfer	Ken	90	90	180
3. Penny Burkeholder	Hope	95	70	165
4. Dodie Green	Roy	89	75	164
5. Bill Berhow	Nick	75	86	161
9. Lewis Burkeholder	Nop	65	88	153

P E N N Y ' S J E A N S were bunched at the waist where her belt had gathered extra cloth and her upper body was lost in a bravely checked flannel cowboy shirt. Her hair was tucked under a fawn gray western hat, shaped into the Tom Mix style.

"I see they haven't forgotten each other." Lewis grinned at Hope and Nop, who were happily renewing their aquaintance.

"Hello, Daddy. How was the drive out? I spent a couple days at Bud Boudreau's place, working Hope on those merino sheep. Those darn things can run like a deer."

"You and that fellow still traveling together?"

"Who? Ransome? No. He cut out on me."

"He special to you?"

181

"I was beginning to think he might be, but I was mistaken. I think Hope's going to win the Finals."

"Uh-huh. Well, your mother and I, we'll be cheering you on. She's really looking forward to seeing you . . . really."

The eyes were sad in Penny's pinched face. "Sure. That'd be great. Look, I got to feed Hope and I should find out about the running order. If you haven't worked these western ewes before, you'd be wise to keep Nop well off."

It wasn't bad advice as advice goes because the first day of the Buffalo trial those wild sheep ran Nop all over the course and he was out of time before he got them penned. Nop's tongue was dragging when he came off the course. The second day he did better, though he wasn't in the money.

Beverly had hoped Penny could spend time with them between the Buffalo trial and the Finals, but as soon as Penny finished on Sunday, she jumped Hope into her Nissan pickup and drove away. Lewis stood in for her at the awards ceremony, accepting her green fifth-place ribbon and check.

When Lewis handed the check to Beverly she made a face. "How does Penny manage?" she asked.

Lewis had been standing around all day and now he itched and was tired and he sprawled in the armchair of their motor home with Nop at his feet. "Penny runs a lot of trials." He unlaced his shoes.

"It would be better if . . . ," Beverly said.

"Yeah, I know," Lewis said. "But she's got her own life to lead. At least we're here to cheer her on."

"Didn't you tell me that Ransome Barlow had a good reputation? You couldn't tell it by the bunch he's running with."

"Miss Ethel said she never saw him touch a drop of whiskey until lately. Boy's got something stuck in his craw. He up and left Penny at some trial out in Washington State and when he returned she wouldn't have a thing to do with him. Do you think we should go home?"

Beverly opened the icebox for an ice tea and poured two glasses. "I've never seen weather like this. One moment it's so warm you can't wear a sweater and next minute you're glad of your earmuffs. I hope it doesn't snow."

"We came out to see Penny," Lewis rolled his glass between his big hands, "but we're no closer to her than if we were back in Virginia. We see her for a few minutes on a trial course and that's that. Beverly, I think we've lost her too."

When Beverly took his wrists, her eyes were hot. "You listen to me, Lewis Burkeholder. There are things about you, I think could be improved. You have a terrible temper. And if you came to church less often, I believe Preacher Shumway would strike you off the rolls. And you haven't a humble bone in your body and, there are things you should be humble about. But the first thing I saw when I met you at that fire department dance, thirty-five years ago, was you weren't going to give up easy. I admired that about you, Lewis. I said to myself then: There are better looking fellows at this dance— Heck, I came with a better looking fellow—but this man will stay with me when things get tough. Now we have driven all the way out here to be with our daughter, Penny, to support her in her bid to be the national champion. She hasn't got any other kin here, so we are it. You trained Nop and trained yourself so we would have a right to be here, on the same field your daughter is on . . ."

"We haven't done much on the field, either."

"Oh, Lewis, honestly, sometimes you make me so mad. Will you listen to yourself?"

Nop put his head on Lewis's knee.

"Well, old-timer, what do you think? You think we got a chance?"

Nop's tail said they did.

"Beverly, I was just thinking. It's a shame to come all this way and not see Yellowstone. We don't need to be in Sheridan until next Friday. Why don't we take a vacation?"

"Do they let dogs in?"

"Beats me. They let bears in."

This late in the season, Yellowstone's campgrounds were almost empty and Lewis and Beverly had their choice of campsites. They walked Nop (on a leash, just like the regulations said) among the emerald pools and the geysers and the mudsprings and bubbling springs.

Lewis and Beverly hadn't taken a vacation together since the year Penny got married, seven years ago. They'd take an early walk and then have a leisurely breakfast and then another walk and lunch and a nap and they'd drive on to a new campground for the night. By week's end they were both relaxed and smiling and several times Nop noticed them walking hand in hand.

A WEEK AGO, MONDAY at sunrise, Penny had pulled into Bob Brennan's place, outside Havre on the Montana Hi-Line. Hope sat upright in the seat next to her.

Bob's wife, Jackie, let the kitchen curtain fall back into place. "That's her. She must have drove all night."

Bob Brennan refolded his *Billings Gazette.* "Yep." He took time to pour himself a cup of coffee before he stepped out onto the porch. "Howdy, Miss Penny. Cold isn't it?"

Penny leaned back, hands on hips, and stretched. Hope watered Brennan's gatepost. "I never saw a place so flat," Penny said.

"When the northers come down from Canada, it can really blow. Step in and get yourself something to eat."

"Hope, you stay with the truck." And she stepped right up to Bob and shook his hand. Funny, she didn't look so little on the trial field. "I passed through some snow outside Cutbank."

"Get inside before we freeze our tails off. Jackie's got your room all fixed up. Our daughter Caroline had it before she went off to the university. I said what was wrong with the college in Havre, but she said she had to go the state university if she wanted to be a psychologist. Told her she'd have all the neighbors for customers. If she could figure why we put up with ranchin', she could make a fortune. Invent some pill—'here, take two'—and get rid of this ranchin' fever."

"I thought ranching was supposed to be romantic."

"Ma'am. I ranched the romance out of the son-of-a-bitch, years ago."

Brennan was a big man, soft around the middle, with a cowboy's skinny behind. Two years ago, he'd been at the Winterfest in Bozeman, Montana, when Bill Berhow put on an exhibition with his Border Collies. He bought a pup from Bill, named it Shep, and now, as they sat around the kitchen table Bob Brennan unfolded Shep's pedigree. Penny showed no more interest in it than Shep did. At Fort Collins Bob had offered Penny $500 for a week of private lessons. He was halfway surprised she'd showed up, but when they took Shep out to the horse corral where Bob kept a dozen practice ewes, Penny was all business. In ten minutes, she had that dog going better than Bob had ever seen him and ten minutes later, when

Shep decided to take a bite of one stubborn ewe, Penny reached out with her shepherd's crook and tapped Shep, just tapped him, on the nose and Shep stopped. "Oh," Shep said, "Something new is required." Bob heard Shep talk, clear as a bell. He wondered why he hadn't heard him before.

That week, every day, they worked Shep in the corral, and morning and afternoon, Bob and Penny rode out over the prairie, and soon as Penny spotted a flock grazing on some distant mesa, Penny sent Shep and thirty minutes later, sometimes forty-five, the sheep were at their feet.

Bob Brennan went on to become a fair dog handler, and he and Shep won several open trials, but he never forgot the slight woman working his dog, better than he could, out in the middle of nowhere; woman, dog, sheep moving with great precision, and she never repeated a request (Bob Brennan couldn't call them commands), and she spoke so soft—just Penny and Shep and the sky, stretching from Canada to Mexico, lighter blue at the rim than in the bowl overhead. Shep never forgot it either.

The second night, Penny moved out of the bedroom back to her camper. She said that sleeping indoors made her uncomfortable, but it wasn't that, it was the ruffled girlishness of the room that oppressed her, like someone was trying to squeeze her into a jar. "It's not your house, Jackie," Penny said, "it's me."

"You got enough blankets?" Jackie asked. "It's below freezing."

In years to come, Jackie and Bob would talk about their guest. Bob would try to explain what happened out there, him and Penny and Shep and usually ended, "I guess you had to be there."

Jackie never would say exactly how she felt—lucky, was part of it; but also ashamed, for some reason, like her life, her ranch, her two kids, hadn't amounted to much, like somehow she might have done something different with her life, something bright and cold and beautiful. Jackie was glad when Friday morning came and Penny left for Sheridan.

Where Ransome Barlow spent the week of the Buffalo trial and the Finals isn't important to our story.

When he pulled into the Equestrian Center at Sheridan, Wyoming, on September twenty-fourth, his entourage of cowboys and down-at-the-heels dog handlers hadn't changed, but Ransome wasn't drinking anymore, not a drop.

NATIONAL HANDLERS' FINALS

꒰ꙮ꒱

1st Qualifying Run
September 25, Sheridan, Wyoming
Judge: Stuart Davidson, Dunoon, Scotland

75 Open dogs went to the post
1. Penny Burkeholder   Hope   93
2. Bill Berhow   Nick   92
3. Candy Kennedy   Sage   92 (Decided on outwork)
4. Ransome Barlow   Bute   90
5. Lewis Burkeholder   Nop   88

THE BANNER over the turnoff to the Sheridan Equestrian Center said: WELCOME TO THE FIFTEENTH ANNUAL NATIONAL HANDLERS' FINALS SHEEPDOG TRIALS. Four o'clock, Friday afternoon, a few handlers gathered in the clubhouse. Others walked the flat trial field. Dogs visited one another among the rows of motor homes. Hope came over to Nop, tail awag, and as befitted the dignity of an Older dog, Nop waited until Hope was close before offering a modest wag of his own. The Bighorn Mountains bulked up behind the field like a shy but determined wall. The lines across the face of the mountains looked like roads, but they were irrigation ditches, passing last winter's snowmelt down to the plains below.

188

When Hope was just six months old, Nop used to take him by the collar and roll him over in the grass while Hope growled fierce as he could. Nop had missed Hope at home, wished there was another dog to walk with and chase foolish squirrels into the air. How *does* a squirrel get from tree to tree?

"How art thou, old man," Hope bowed and yawned.

Nop inspected the course, self-importantly. "Thou hast learned nothing since last I dragged your collar," he said.

Hope grinned at him. "Tomorrow I shall work woolies. Tomorrow and the day after. Oh, I am a fine stockdog."

Nop grumbled, "There's more to life than that."

"What? What more pray? Me and my woman, we go out, we make the woolies dance. She is wise. She says good words when we talk."

"It is unwise to talk to them," the older dog grumbled. "When we talk, they learn more about us than is proper."

But the young dog wandered over where the pipe was flooding into the irrigation ditch below the clubhouse and, ears cocked, inspected the spot where the earth squirted water.

The trial organizers had laid out finger food in the clubhouse, some handlers hung on the cash bar, some inspected the art works hanging for a silent auction, while others ate on the deck, admiring the mountains.

"It's so pretty out here," Beverly said.

"Are you cold? Do you want to go inside?"

Penny slapped a taco on a paper plate, got a cup of black coffee, added four packets of sugar and came out onto the deck.

"Would you fetch me my sweater, Lewis?" Beverly asked.

Enroute to the motor home, Lewis spotted Hope and Old Nop snuffling along the bank of the irrigation ditch, and as the younger dog effortlessly vaulted across, Nop hesitated. Lewis winced.

Beverly loomed over her daughter until Penny raised her eyes. "We haven't talked," Beverly said. "Don't you think we should?"

Though Penny hadn't taken three bites, she tossed her plate in the trashbasket and wiped her hands.

The way Penny brushed the hair out of her eyes—when had she become a wife, mother, widow? But Penny's gaze was as bleak as those blue mountains. Beverly hadn't seen that gaze before. "Talk doesn't help," Penny said.

"Baby"—Beverly hadn't meant to say that—"can't we try? It makes us heartsick, me and your Daddy, to see you so alone."

Penny managed a shakey grin. "So long as I got Hope, I'm not alone. You know how far we come, in just one year? Oh I've heard people talking: Hope's too young, too inexperienced for the pressure. If I was a man, they wouldn't be talking that way."

"Penny . . ."

"I'm glad to see you and Daddy here. I didn't think you'd come. I never meant to hurt you."

"Honey, we were hoping you'd come back to Virginia with us after the Finals. Lewis says there's no more trials to speak of until the new year."

"No more big trials, maybe. But there's clinics and private lessons." Penny's voice lowered. "Ma, I just can't bear to live my old life. Me and Hope are building a new one."

Beverly was glad it was getting dark and nobody could see she was crying. She plunged into her purse for a tissue. When a voice said, "Hello Penny, you've done a job this year," Beverly turned to the newcomer with relief, and Penny introduced them.

Oren Wright was quick to touch the brim of his Stetson, say "ma'am," but his eyes were on Penny all the time, and Beverly felt a twinge of jealousy for the child that had once been hers alone. "I came to offer you a job," he said.

Penny produced a wan smile. "You came all the way out here to say that? You might have telephoned."

"And you might have told me no. My Uncle Nick had several of those frequent flier passes. So long as I answer 'Here Sir' whenever the airline asks which passenger is Nick Wright, I can fly for free. And I asked for the handler's rate at the Holiday Inn, and they gave it to me, just like I was a sheepdog champion. I don't know if you been to that Holiday Inn yet, but they've got a waterfall right in the lobby. The Holiday Inn's where they're going to have the Handlers' Banquet Saturday night. You all buy your tickets?"

Beverly said, "Will you come with us, Penny?"

Penny closed her eyes. "Ma, I hate those things."

Beverly stayed quite still. Didn't move a muscle.

"Sure," Penny said, "You bet. I'll buy my own ticket. Now if you two will excuse me, I've got to find Hope before he wanders off."

Beverly murmured, "Dear God, I am so frightened for her."

"That girl's tougher than she looks," Oren said just as softly.

"I'm afraid she's not," Beverly said. "And she hasn't got a soul to care for her except a dog." She put on a bright smile and said, "Mister Wright, my husband has got off somewhere to fetch me a wrap. It certainly gets chilly here when the sun

191

goes down. I wonder if you'd be good enough to bring me a, oh, a bourbon and Coke would be nice. I haven't had one of those in years."

And when Lewis came back with Beverly's jacket—he hadn't been able to find her sweater—he draped it over her shoulders, and took a sip of her drink, said, "Beverly!"

"Well, this nice Mr. Wright was kind enough to get it for me. Lewis, he runs three thousand ewes. Penny lambed out for him last spring."

Penny ran well the next morning. On spooky sheep, Hope never set a paw wrong. Nop's sheep were more difficult, but the old dog stayed back off them, never forced the pace, and Lewis finished the course with seconds to spare.

None of Ransome Barlow's roughneck buddies finished in the top ten—only one scooted into the top twenty. They bitched about the judging and drank beer.

That night, Ethel Harwood took Lewis and Beverly to dinner at the Wagon Box Inn, which was near the site of an 1870s Indian fight. Like most good restaurants in Wyoming, the Wagon Box was a steak house, log walls, big solid tables, prime rib if you didn't like steak.

Ethel had her gin and tonic, Lewis wanted a beer, and Beverly ordered hot tea.

When the waitress brought their bread basket, Beverly bowed her head and thanked God for the food and their good friends and prayed that Penny would soon be her old self again. Ethel Harwood coughed and drank most of her gin and tonic.

"You know," Lewis said, "it's strange to come out here and think that it was the same soldiers fought the Indians as fought my grandparents. In 1864, when Sheridan came down the Shenandoah Valley he burnt and destroyed everything:

192

barns, cattle, wheat, corn shucks, everything, and Custer was Sheridan's man. It was General Custer burned our barn. Those old silo foundations behind the Harvestore, is where it was. On the way over from Yellowstone me and Beverly stopped at the Custer battlefield and I stood over Custer's grave and I couldn't help myself from thinking: It serves you right."

Beverly looked up from her menu. "Oh, there's that nice young man Penny worked for. Lewis, shouldn't we invite him to join us?"

"You're becoming a regular fan of these sheepdog trials, Mr. Wright," Lewis said.

"I could bring you your salad now," the waitress said, "while you look over the menu."

Oren Wright said, "Just burn me a steak, rib eye, home fries, cup of coffee." And he handed back his menu. "I never saw a good dog until Penny came to work for me. That dog saved us a full-time hired man."

"Maybe Penny ought to ask wages for Hope," Lewis said.

"Why do you do it? Why do you take all the time, travel so far, just to compete in a sheepdog trial?"

Beverly helped Lewis out. "It's just something to occupy your mind."

"It comes over you like a sickness," Lewis said. "When I started with the Stink Dog, twenty years ago, I soon couldn't get enough of it. I put twenty thousand miles on my pickup that year, going to dog trials. It's a wonder Beverly didn't divorce me."

"I considered it," Beverly said but took the sting away by patting his hand.

Ethel said, "At home, I just fix myself a breast of chicken or a little fish or, sometimes, just a vegetable casserole. Since we've been out west I've been eating beef until it comes out of my ears."

But despite Ethel's grumbling she ate hearty, and when the waitress brought coffee, they asked for doggy bags, real doggy bags, and Oren's bones went into Ethel's bag, and Beverly and Lewis pooled theirs for Nop.

Lewis leaned forward: "When me and Nop are out there, oh, it's like sometimes we're so close I can feel every slowness in that old dog, like it was my own slowness. He and me are the same animal. If I'm confused, he's confused. If he can't find his sheep, I can't do a thing. If I misjudge a gate and he misses it, it's like I failed him. There's all sorts of fellows run these dogs, and maybe some of those fellows aren't nice natured, but I never met a one who didn't talk about the gratitude he feels toward his dogs. Oh, I been out in *some* weather with that dog." Lewis coughed and turned beet red and took a drink of water, and Ethel Harwood said it was the nicest dinner she'd had since she was in Wyoming, that it had made her less homesick.

September 26, Sheridan, Wyoming
Judge: Stuart Davidson, Dunoon, Scotland

75 Open dogs went to the post			Cumulative
1. Penny Burkeholder	Hope	94	187
2. Ransome Barlow	Bute	92	184
3. Bruce Fogt	Molly	89	171
4. Lewis Burkeholder	Nop	88	172
5. Bill Berhow	Nick	87	179

THE SECOND DAY of qualifying was bitter cold and the wind gusted off the Bighorns and some dogs couldn't hear the whistles. The T-shirt concessionaires moved inside the clubhouse and looked glumly at the empty grandstands. The Buffalo Burger concession closed its shutters after lunch, and the cook at the Cowboy Chuckwagon never took off his down jacket all day. One by one the dogs made their runs and only the hard-core handlers sat in lawn chairs, wrapped in blankets watching them.

Handlers who'd rented rooms at the Holiday Inn were under seige from the motorhome campers who took this occasion to go in for a shower. Some Holiday Inn rooms went through ten or twelve towels that day.

Ransome Barlow lost most of his points at the shed: Bute couldn't keep the sheep in the shedding ring.

Dark clouds over the Bighorns were punctured by light when Penny and Hope went to the post. Watching her, Beverly wondered where her daughter washed her hair.

Penny was so light, so fey, she was like a sprite. But Hope was a young dog with all a young dog's ways, hearty and bouncy, and when he dropped to the ground, his front went down first and then his back in a slow stage collapse, tail last of all. The fence was lined with handlers, and everybody who'd brought a camera had it in their hands. Penny slightly misjudged the crossdrive gate but otherwise it was a perfect run until the pen, when one of the ewes turned and pawed the ground and Hope hesitated before he came on again and backed his sheep into the pen. Applause in the chilly air.

Ransome sent Bute to take the sheep off the course. Bute's sudden arrival confused Hope, and two dogs made more work of it than one dog might have.

When Penny walked by Ransome she snapped, "I don't need your help."

Ransome felt ill done by. Hadn't he tracked down Marvin and P.T. for her? And if it hadn't turned out exactly the way he'd hoped, hadn't he got even for her? When he came back, brought their pickup to the Fort Collins trial, he meant to tell her what he'd done, had meant to tell her she had nothing to fear from those two hombres anymore, but she'd jumped on him so quick and so hot, accused him of leaving her stranded, accused him of running out on her, that his mouth jammed up and he couldn't utter a word until it was long past too late.

Ransome drawled, "I was afraid that weak dog of yours couldn't get them off the course."

"I don't need your interfering," Penny said. "I never asked help from you and I'm not starting today."

Ransome was under the impression that she'd asked him for a good deal of help over the last months. "That dog's weak as water," he said. "Every trial he runs more scared."

Hope had tucked himself behind Penny's leg, and she felt his pressure like a great obligation. "He seems to beat you regular," she said, feeling as she spoke that her words were helpless, feminine: not enough.

The bile rose in Ransome's throat. He swallowed. He looked at the mountain peaks. Some wind must have got into his eyes, left him feeling soft and bleak, like nothing he'd done in his life had been any account and nothing much would be. Him and her—what a silly, silly, silly idea. Down the field a busted-down cowpoke was putting out sheep for the dogs. That'd be him one year. Except for his animals, he'd be alone. "Some of us going over to the Ag Station tonight to work our dogs on some tough sheep, see what they can do."

"I bought a ticket for the banquet." Hope leaned hard against Penny's leg. It was a wonder she could bear his heavy, furry weight.

"Hell. Banquet's just a bunch of speeches from fellows don't commonly make speeches about how terrific we all are. I already know I'm terrific." He tried a grin but couldn't quite bring it off. "Hell," he said, "go to the banquet if that's what you want. Me, I got a real dog to train."

Penny felt loosened from the earth, everything at risk and

flying. She'd take whatever magic was offered her. "Done. But I got to let my Mom know."

Half an hour later, Beverly said, "I'm sorry you're not feeling well, honey. Maybe we could all skip the banquet, go out someplace quiet. Tonight—"

"I know what tonight is! I can handle it. Best part of a year, I've been handling it. You know what tomorrow's going to be, Ma? It'll be the day me and Hope win our first National Handlers' Finals. That's what tomorrow will be, nothing else, just that."

Beverly's eyes were too soft but that may have been on account of the fading light. It was six-thirty and people were leaving for the banquet. A few had their headlights on. "We'll always be here for you," she said, "Lewis and me. You can come home any time or telephone us and we'll come and fetch you." And the two women fell into each others arms until Beverly patted her daughter briskly on the back and drew away. "My, aren't we a pair. It's time for me to clean up. God bless you, honey."

Behind the grandstand, the Cowboy Chuckwagon cook put the day's receipts in a green canvas bag. To his wife he said, "I suppose it could have been worse. We aren't going to get any crowd tomorrow if it snows."

At the banquet, under the banner *15th Annual National Finals—Purina is Proud to Sponsor the Handlers' Finals,* Judge Davidson and his wife sat with association officials and their wives. The trophies were nearby, on a velvet-covered podium: the big Handlers' Association shield, smaller trophies for the best qualifying runs, the glitter of silver trays.

Everybody wore their Saturday night best: western shirts, corduroy jackets, string ties. Even Nathan Mooney was wearing a tie. Before anybody ate, Lewis Pulfer stood and offered grace, and Beverly bowed her head and put out her hands and their table was soon linked by clasped hands. When Lewis said, "Amen," the room chatter resumed.

"I don't see Ransome Barlow here tonight," Ethel Harwood said. "Nor his pals. Why in the world fellas like that want to get involved with sheepdogs . . ." Beverly was picking at her food and Lewis was beginning to think that Penny'd made the right decision not coming tonight.

Nathan Mooney made a short speech, thanking all the people who'd done so much to make the trial a success and announcing that they had a trophy to award to the most promising new handler, a handler who was attending the Nationals for the very first time. "And the most promising new handler is Miz Penny Burkeholder with her dog, Hope. Penny, you here tonight?"

As Lewis walked through the patter of applause to collect Penny's trophy, Nathan said the Burkeholders were a real sheepdog family, that the Burkeholders were the only family to have two people qualify for the top fifteen who'd run tomorrow, and since he'd already given that much away he might as well announce the official qualifiers, that the fifteenth dog was Red Oliver, with Roy. Applause after each name and Lewis was surprised to find himself fourth place overall, after Penny, Ransome, and Bill Berhow. "Nice going, honey," said Beverly, patting his arm.

On the podium, Herbert Holmes explained that this year's Calcutta paid to four places, not a cumulative score, *repeat,* only the top four scores *tomorrow,* and then Herbert was auctioneering, crying up the prices. "Red Oliver from Texas and Roy, do I hear fifty dollars, fifty, fifty, fifty, fifty-five, now sixty, thank you," and the spotters cried up the bidders and the Scottish judge shook his head in wonder.

Ethel Harwood "bought" Lewis for $320. Ransome fetched nearly $500, and Herbert started the bidding for Penny at $500. "Five, five, five, do I hear five, thank you, Lewis, five-fifty, do I hear five-fifty. Yes! The young man sitting with the Burkeholders. Lewis, will you go six, six, six. Five seventy-five then. I've got five seventy-five, do I hear six . . ."

Oren bid Lewis up to $800, which was an all-time record for the Handlers' Calcutta. Lewis's stoney face broke into a grin, and he reached across the table to shake the younger man's hand. "Thanks for turnin' loose of me. I would have gone on forever."

"Now come up here to the head table and hand your money to our secretary here," Herbert said. "And for the rest of you, we've got a good cowboy dance band here tonight, so you all stay as late as you want and have a good time."

Herbert Holmes was first out on the floor with the judge's wife. Oren offered to partner Beverly Burkeholder, but Beverly said, "Not tonight, thanks so much. I think Lewis and I'll go back to our motor home. It sure was nice eating with you."

Lewis shook a few hands, said a few "See you tomorrows," and the couple went through the motel lobby, where they'd turned off the waterfall. It had cleared outside, the clouds blown away, and Lewis said, "Beverly, I believe that's the dog star. You think that's good luck?"

She linked her arm in his. "No matter how it turns out," she said softly, "I'm glad I came."

. . .

It's HARD to ruin a good dog. Dog trainers who salvage diso-
bedient family pets—re-creating in the dog an image of a good
dog—sometimes tell you a dog can never be ruined: hurt yes,
discouraged, yes, but no dog, they say, is irreparable. This
article of faith is both brave and necessary, but the dogs that
come to them have been damaged by the ignorant.

People often wonder just what trainers give the sheepdog
in exchange for its boundless willingness. Food treats and
praise sit on the trainer's shelf, untouched, unused. The sheepdog is shown its possibilities, he learns what life is like for a
good dog and is invited to walk in a rational world whose
farthest boundaries are defined by grace.

There are dog saints as there are human saints. And a saint
is a saint because his faith cannot be broken. A young dog's
faith is absolute—he literally cannot imagine how he could be
other than he is. A young dog has never seen hell. It takes a
wonderful trainer to show it to him.

THE SKY WAS BLACK and rolling. The alfalfa fields beside the
road were achingly green. The dead range grass was blond as a
young girl's hair. Part of Penny noticed the wonderful light
that hovered between clouds and earth, and part of her thought
it didn't make any difference.

The road climbed into the low hills, past the irrigated fields
onto pure rangeland. Where the road crested, Penny could see
fifty or sixty miles, rolling seered hills, grass, rimrocks, and
ridges. One of Ransome's buddies led the caravan, ten pickups
in a row, license plates from all over the country.

Penny passed the historical marker for the Fetterman Mas-
sacre, the rock spire that identified the spot where eighty cav-

alrymen under Captain Fetterman failed to make good his boast that he could, with a handful of troopers, ride right through the entire Sioux Nation. It is easier to sacrifice others if we don't much care what happens to ourselves.

Penny checked her trip odometer. "Five more miles and I'm gonna turn around."

Hope thumped his tail, but Penny didn't respond to his remark.

Four and a half miles later, as Penny was watching for a wide spot where she could turn, the lead pickup flipped its blinkers, and soon enough the entire line blinked as one: left, left, going left soon.

It was the John Douglass Agricultural Research Station, and the road was a lane and a half, nicely graveled and graded. You could see the whole spread; the light glistening off the care-taker's white trailer and the pole barn's roof shiny as tin foil. A rail fence outlined the parking lot behind the barn, and as they pulled up, the trailer opened, backlighting the cowboy in the entryway. He held a bowl and was scooping food into his mouth.

Penny got out to pull on her down jacket. Ransome Barlow said, "Smells like snow."

The caretaker was wizened, somewhere between fifty and seventy. He slipped a loaded spoon under his stained white mustache and brought it out shiny. "I didn't think you'd show," he said.

"Couldn't keep us away from it," Ransome said with something like a smile. "Heard you got some tough sheep up here? We got some dogs for 'em, just the ticket."

The cowboy set his bowl on a gatepost.

Suffolk rams are big, some well over three hundred

pounds, and every few days, men had caught these rams and stuck needles in them to draw blood for hemophilia research and for ovine research and to teach clumsy vet students how to draw blood. These rams were mad.

The lot behind the pole barn was twelve acres, falling away from the barn's doors. The mercury vapor lights cast a blue light. The fence was high tensile wire, ten strand, strong enough to hold horses.

Penny kept her hands in her pockets and tried not to shiver as three men and their dogs went inside the barn after the rams. At the bottom of the pasture a handler waited, ready to train his dog. A tremendous commotion inside, heavy objects thumped the walls, a dog yelped, and four rams burst out of the barn, and before the man at the door could close it, smashed back inside.

Ransome turned to Penny. "Do you think your dog can bring them out of there?" he asked. "Get 'em a hundred yards out in the lot and we can work them."

Without a word, Penny started for the barn where the bumping continued and one dog was barking, yip, yip, yip.

Inside, Penny found two men dragging a ram, one on each hind leg while a third man waited to slide the door open.

One dog had climbed a loaded hay wagon, another was atop the automatic feeders, a third yipped from the space underneath a stocktub. The men were grunting and sweating and one man delivered a kick as he rolled the sheep out the door.

Penny stood aside while they dragged two more sheep out.

The man sliding the door had buttons gone from his shirt. "You puttin' 'em out? Good luck!"

Penny said something to her dog. The three rams clung to

the safety of the barn door and Hope ran in to peel them away. Startled by Hope's sudden appearance the rams jumped a few yards down the hill and Hope swung behind them, smooth as glass, but the sheep leader saw the men waiting—*for me?*—and spun and charged and Hope leapt to meet him, bit him on the nose, once, twice, and the ram shook his head and trotted downhill, and his companions followed.

The handler at the bottom sent his dog, which gathered the sheep, fetched them to his master, and then the sheep panicked and bolted straight for the barn, and Hope raced to intercept them, keep them in the field.

With Hope between the sheep and the barn, it was barely possible to work a dog. The sheep paid no attention to the dogs unless they nipped, and when they nipped, the sheep bolted back to the barn until Hope intercepted them.

Hope faced three-hundred-pound rams with his will, his glare, his attitude, and sometimes, his teeth.

The barn men changed the sheep, brought out new ones, but they were no different.

The world outside that lighted pasture went dark and it was a stage with crazy animals facing Hope, weaving and bobbing.

Penny thought: They aren't going to beat me.

Hope thought: Oh, they come, they come and again they come, and I turn them and again they come. Is this the world? Is this how it is for me? He asked Penny for help, but she wasn't listening.

At Penny's command Hope faced the enormous hysterical animals and time after time Hope stopped them, and some of Ransome's buddies got disgusted and quit but others waited because they hadn't had their turn and fair is fair.

Hope begged Penny, but she couldn't hear what he said.

Penny thought: They can't do this to me.

When a ram broke past Hope and crashed into the barn door trying to burst through to shelter, Penny kicked it, and Hope read that as a command he should attack, so he gripped the ram's wool and hung on, like a forty-pound sea anchor.

"Turn loose of him Hope, damn you, damn you," Penny screamed.

Hope thought: I am mistaken. I have betrayed her. He let go and the ram ran over him. When he scrambled to his feet, he couldn't look at Penny, fearing what he'd see there. He asked himself: Who am I?

The sheep became the mindless creatures most people think they are. They became their terrified impulse to hide themselves back in the barn where nothing could get to them.

"Ransome, you gonna work Bute?"

"Nope," Ransome said. Under the bleak lights Penny and Hope fought those rams: meat and muscle, heads lowered to butt.

None of the handlers were trying to work their dogs anymore, they just watched the hopeless crazy fight, and when a ram knocked Penny off her feet nobody laughed, and when Hope grabbed a ram nobody cried out.

Ransome turned away. "I'm goin' down the road."

"We gonna see you later? Have a few beers?"

Ransome never looked back.

The rams came at Hope full tilt, and he leapt to meet them and was smashed off his feet and the woman was screaming something, some command that made no sense now and probably never had.

. . .

THE NATIONAL FINALS had been featured in the *Billings Gazette* and all the Wyoming papers. Since Sunday dawn broke warm and seasonal, several thousand Wyoming stockmen and women decided to come out and see what a really well-trained dog could do. Most drove pickups; a few Cadillacs and Continentals nosed in among the trucks, but not many Mercedes or Volvos.

Ranch Border Collies hopped out of the back of pickups to chat with trial Border Collies as the announcer explained the course, said that every competitor was a champion, said there'd be special events on the grounds all day, said they should get a Buffalo Burger if they were hungry.

Lewis Burkeholder wore his whipcord trousers and sport jacket, his go-to-church tie, his dress Stetson, so white it sparkled. Beverly was dressed in a tailored green suit. Lewis had bought her a flower at the Holiday Inn this morning, a small purple orchid, and she had it pinned to her lapel. Several times that morning, Penny's parents walked past Penny's pickup, but though Hope was chained underneath the truck, the camper was closed up tight and there was no sign of Penny.

"Handlers' meeting. Will the top fifteen competitors meet with the judge?"

The course had grown bigger since the qualifying runs, the crossdrive stretched out five hundred yards wide and the outrun was nearly a mile.

"After the fetch," the judge said, in his soft Scottish burr, "it'll be different than yesterday. Today you'll do a double lift. Stop your dog when he's brought his sheep through the fetch gates, then send him off again, over there, make another outrun to pick up his second lot. When you've joined both lots, you can do your drive and crossdrive, same as yesterday, only bigger don't you see, and then you'll bring fifteen sheep into the shedding ring and shed off the five with ribbons around their necks, take them to the pen, quite simple, yes? Any questions?"

Somebody asked, "When's the next plane out of here?"

When Penny crawled out of her camper, she wore the jeans and shirt she'd worn the night before. One knee was smeared black, the seat of her pants was dirty and an elbow was out of her shirt.

Although Hope whined to be let loose, she ignored him, carried a suitcase to Ethel Harwood's camper and asked could she come inside and change.

"Sure, honey. You want a shower? I filled up the tank last night. You feelin' all right, you look awfully pale?"

Penny washed her face and brushed her hair and said no, she didn't want any coffee, would it be all right if she used the toilet. After she closed the door, Ethel heard her retching.

She was paper white when she came out.

"Hope feeling ready this morning?"

"That's up to him, isn't it? It's been one year today," Penny said. "Since Mark and Lisa died."

Ethel wanted to hug her, but Penny held her body so brittle and aloof.

Penny brought Hope on a lead, like he was a wild dog, a pet dog, a dog that didn't know any better. She led him across the irrigation ditch to do his business, which he did, facing away from her. He didn't paw dirt over his scat, didn't trot away, tail in a plume, didn't look at her, said nothing. "Hope, come to me. Hope! You come to me, you!"

One step at a time, like he was dragged; his chest rose and fell with each breath.

"I'm sorry, Hope. I, just don't know how I . . . God, I'm sorry."

Hope snuffled a tumbleweed, lifted his leg.

"You're gonna be fine, aren't you? Soon as you go out on that course, it'll be you and me, just like we always was. Hope, I wasn't there when my baby died. I couldn't stand it if I hurt you too." She gripped his head and tried to look into his eyes but he jerked away from her.

"A very nice job by Dodie Green" the announcer said. "Just a little trouble at the shed. Next up, Charles O'Reilly, from Red Wing, Minnesota, with his fine dog, Shep, trying to work these wild Wyoming sheep out here on this tough, tough course. Every one of the dogs that runs today is already a champion."

It was a brilliant day, the last fine day of Indian summer. Behind the grandstands, Basque children danced the dances their parents brought when they'd come to this strange country to be shepherds. Accordian, fiddle, four children in green and black folk costumes. Camera flashes blinked in the sunlight.

A few handlers removed their dogs' collars before they walked onto the course, telling the dog the connection between them had nothing to do with leather and steel. Empty dog collars dangled from the fence while great dogs made their try.

Cowboys and ranchers watched from pickups or in the bleachers or perched on the fenders of their cars. The sheep were going well, the two days of qualifications had accustomed them to dogs and the dogs had learned their ways, and despite the enlarged course size, things were going smoothly.

"Congratulations," Lewis Burkeholder said to his daughter. She looked blank. "For winning best newcomer. Honey, I'm proud of you."

And Penny dropped her head and hurried right by. Lewis couldn't remember when he'd seen Hope on a leash.

Penny and Hope hid out in the clubhouse. The silent auction had failed to draw many bids, and only a few of the artworks bore tiny red SOLD stickers. One painting depicted a dog with Hope's markings approaching two lost lambs while, the sheepherder followed the dog from horseback. The artist had known dogs and sheep and loved them, and Penny wished somebody had put a bid on it, but love and skill don't necessarily mean very much, she thought, it's luck you need. Hope faced into the corner, where nothing or nobody could get at him. "The work will put you right," Penny said aloud, and a woman inspecting the paintings turned, startled, and Penny put on a ghastly smile and said, "Talkin' to m'dog."

The woman had a weather-beaten face, and her jeans and her shirt were fresh and her boots so new the soles still had their original finish. "You run that dog in this trial?" she asked.

"I got started a year ago."

"We bought our first dog six months ago. We handle cattle from horseback but we needed a dog for the goats. You just can't rope a goat." She grinned. "Honey, you okay?"

Penny went into her pocket for her red and black checked handkerchief. "I was thinking of something else," she said. "But I can't think about that right now, I got to get through this Final today, then I'll be okay."

The cowgirl was older than Penny, ten years or so. "Here I am pestering you and you want to be alone, you and your dog. Hell, I'm sorry."

Penny said, "No, it's not that. You got kids?"

The woman sighed and looked out the clubhouse windows. Bar X Ropes had a roping dummy outside its tent that kids

209

were trying to lasso. "Hank and me, we can't have kids," she said. "He's got a daughter from a first marriage but I had an infection and got my tubes tied. Daughter comes up and visits us in the summer months. She left last week to go home to California to learn how to shop. I surely miss that child." She paused, "You?"

Penny shook her head. No, she didn't have any children, never had had a daughter named Lisa. "What I got is this dog."

"That'd be too lonesome for me," the woman said. "I go to bed, it's snowing outside, I like to crawl right up against my Hank. Maybe he doesn't shave often as he should and sometimes his breath stinks of whiskey but, by God, he's warm."

Penny blew her nose. "Thanks." She said, "I enjoyed talking to you. I got to go now, check out the course."

"You really okay, honey?"

Penny glared. " 'Course I am. Me and Hope, we gonna win this goddamned thing." And she gave a jerk on the lead and Hope followed her out of the clubhouse like a barge after a tug.

"I'll be rootin' for you," the cowgirl called after her.

On the course Ransome Barlow was having the run of a lifetime. He got a tremendous round of applause when he and Bute walked off the course, and Ransome swept his black hat to the earth in thanks. Of 120 possible points, on that big course, he'd managed 104. Ransome felt like he weighed about twenty pounds, like he literally might float off the earth, and he scarcely heard the congratulations as he walked toward his pickup.

"All the dogs here today are champions," the announcer said, "but the dog who wins this today will be a champion of champions. Don't forget we've got folk dancing in front of the clubhouse. Go on over and give the kids some support."

Ransome had good intentions when he approached Penny. "Sorry about last night," he said. "If I'd known those sheep were that rank, I wouldn't have invited you."

Penny said, "It doesn't make any difference."

Hope was at the fence, bored, as if nothing on the course interested him in the slightest.

Ransome winced. "To him it does. Did you see the way Ol' Bute did that second lift? Ever seen anything so pretty?"

Penny shrugged.

"I suppose you're gonna beat us?"

And she faced him with her red-rimmed eyes and said, "Why not? Me and Hope been whippin' you all summer."

It was like somebody kicked Ransome in the stomach. Suddenly he was so overwhelmingly angry that he turned away. He knew, in that instant, why it is that guns kill people: because they are quicker than our remorse. "I don't suppose you'd like to put your money where your mouth is," he said.

"You never paid me for my half of the pickup."

Ransome breathed in and out, in and out. "Okay," he said. "That's the way you want it. Dog against dog. You go out there and get a better score than Bute—that's today—no cumulative score, just today, and I'll sign his registration over to you. I beat you, I take Hope."

And suddenly, alarmingly, she smiled, and it was a sunny smile, no hurt in it, the smile of a young girl who sees nothing wrong in the world because she has found love. She knelt down beside the dog. "How about it Hopey? Can we beat those two? Just like always—we'll go out there and do it?" Her joy beamed

211

over Ransome. "Hopey says 'sure.' Hopey says he can do it. You just go get your papers ready, because we're going to go out there and make everything right."

Ransome felt sick to his stomach—all that adrenaline pulsing through him—and his heart stuffed his throat so full he couldn't talk. He nodded to seal the bargain.

AT NOON, they broke for half an hour. The announcer talked. He talked about the sponsors; the Cowboy Roundup Sheepdog Committee who were putting on this great trial; the fact that every dog here was already a champion; how useful these dogs were on ranches and farms. But as he was talking, the news of Ransome's wager flashed through the handlers; heads turning to listen, twosomes and threesomes forming and breaking up. Lewis closed his eyes and the fellow who'd given him the news asked, "Lewis, you okay?"

"Yeah. Oh, mercy." Lewis turned as his wife of so many years hurried toward him.

"Lewis, what is that girl trying to prove?"

"I believe she's bettin' the pot," he said.

It was one-thirty on a shadowless September afternoon when Penny Burkeholder and Hope walked onto the course of the most important sheepdog trial in North America. They'd worked all year to get here, ran trial after trial, learning the arts and trust of trailing. They had a ten-point lead going in and would win today if the spread between them and Ransome Barlow stayed the same, though of course, they had to beat him outright today to win her bet.

Big as the field was, it was easier to see the mounted cowboys putting out sheep than the sheep themselves.

Penny walked as if each step was being scored. Hope followed dolefully on his lead, looking at the ground. She stooped and unclipped him, and Hope jumped ten feet away. She called him and laid him down and leaned over him, talking and talking and talking. One rancher asked when she was going to begin and a handler said, "The clock doesn't start running until she sends him."

On the sidelines, Lewis Burkeholder could not look away. At his side, his good wife had her head bowed and her eyes closed. Lewis felt fragile. He remembered a verse the preacher had read at Mark and Lisa's funeral service, how life is labour and sorrow, we are soon cut off and we fly away.

The dog sailed out to the left, just fine and the announcer —who'd heard about the wager—covered the mike with his hand, "Might be that girl'll have two dogs to take home tonight."

Out he went, out, out, and Penny poised at the handler's stake, ready to guide him or give advice whenever he might need it. The crowd could see the cowboys on horseback trotting away from the sheep and then, the sheep came, and for the first bit it was fine, but then the sheep started to speed up, and Penny blew her whistle, "Hope, take time!" but the sheep came on quicker, at a gallop now, this dog right at their heels and no telling what he had in mind. Once again, Penny told Hope to take time, but on came the sheep, legs stretched in a gallop in a mob, and a mob can't all fit through the gates and Penny told Hope to STOP, to LIE DOWN and on they came, around the side of the gate. Hope laid down. The sheep slowed and drifted of their own accord to the spot where they should be. Next the handler is supposed to send the dog to a second bunch, half a mile out, ninety degrees west. The double lift has been called a crisis of faith, and it is. For a dog it's like changing careers in midlife.

Penny told Hope to LOOK BACK! Hope ignored her, concentrated on the sheep he had and started pushing them across the course, thud, thud, thud, deliberate as a locomotive. Penny whistled him down. He ignored her. She whistled him down. He ignored her. His feet like pistons, up down, up down.

She whistled him down. She whistled him down. She whistled a recall a "That'll do, here!" She whistled him down.

The sheep marched away from the crowd, the pickups, the judge, the woman, toward the Bighorns.

"Hope there's a fence out there," someone said.

"Christ," someone else said.

Ransome Barlow turned his back.

Penny Burkeholder cried, "Lisa, don't!"

A Wyoming rancher turned to a Virginia handler. "I thought her dog's name was Hope," he said.

The Virginian said, "That's right." He added, "I think it's time to get a cup of coffee. You want one?"

The judge was standing on the very edge of his stand. Sometimes you saw this sort of thing with young dogs at nursery trials, but this was the National Finals.

Penny had quit commanding, stood silent as a strange dog did whatever was on its mind.

Hope thought, "I am not Hope, I am not him. Move woolies."

The president of the Handlers' Association hurried onto the judge's platform and the two men conferred. The judge called out, "That'll do, Ms. Burkeholder. Call your dog."

Hope pushed the sheep relentlessly west.

A second time, the judge called, "Ms. Burkeholder, that'll do. Will you please fetch your dog?"

The announcer chimed in, "Well that's tough luck for Penny Burkeholder and her dog, Hope. Disqualified for going 'off course.' Next handler will be Bill Berhow with Nick. Bill's from Lavina, Monatana, not many miles from here . . ."

As the pickup man sent his dog out to get Hope's sheep, Lewis Burkeholder jogged onto the course. Lewis wrapped his jacket around his daughter's shoulders.

When the pickup dog came around Hope's sheep, Hope whipped to the far side to cancel the other dog's effort and the sheep kept on drifting in the same direction, more nervously, since now there were two dogs.

Most country people are deeply polite and nobody was waiting for Penny and her father at the gate except Beverly. Nobody was standing nearby; the nearest handlers faced away, deep in private conversations, and the Burkeholders passed invisibly.

Two more pickup dogs were trying to bring the sheep off but Hope, darting back and forth, balanced fifteen sheep and three good dogs and kept the sheep marching toward the Bighorns.

From the judge's platform, the president called: "Lewis, didn't this dog used to be yours?"

"I'll take care of Penny," Beverly said, and mother and daughter passed to the motor home through a crowd of sudden strangers.

On the course, three dogs and one cowboy were working to bring the sheep in, but Hope was a whirlwind, and what was meant to be the most serious test of the sheepdog's art was

threatening to turn funny. Some of the cowboys on the sidelines were rooting for Hope: underdog.

And in its own crazy way, it was beautiful: one dog defying
fifteen sheep, three dogs, a man on horseback, and now three
men on foot. And he was quicker than the men on foot, more
agile than the rider, who was being loudly advised to "dab a
loop on him, cowpoke." And the cowboy was reaching for his
lariat when Lewis arrived, said "Hope, that'll do."

And Hope followed Lewis off the course, wagging his tail
like "Haven't I done good, wasn't that fun?" Foolish as a
puppy.

The crowd applauded Lewis and maybe Hope too, but
Lewis didn't doff his cap because he was ashamed and didn't
see anything funny at all.

He fastened Hope to Penny's truck and the dog squirmed
underneath.

When Lewis rapped at his motor home door Beverly stuck
her head out and gave him the look that meant "not now," so
Lewis waited in Ethel Harwood's motor home.

A full hour later, Beverly knocked and Ethel said, "I guess
I'll go get me something to eat, you hungry?" Which they
weren't, nor was Ethel particularly.

"She cried herself to sleep. I didn't think she'd ever stop.
Lisa, how she blames herself. If she'd been there with her,
maybe she could have got Lisa out. She blames Mark too, for
taking Lisa with him that day and having the accident. You
know what is worst for Penny? How afraid Lisa must have
been, underwater, her daddy holding her up in the air and his
arms losing their strength. We prayed together, for Lisa and
Mark. Penny said she ruined her dog. Can you do that, Lewis,
can you really ruin them?"

"Reckon you can."

"Penny says she wants to go home with us."

"Well, that's what we wanted."

"Yes," she said, "I do."

Lewis took a sip of ice tea and said, "I believe she truly loves that dog."

Beverly said, "Maybe you can find her another one."

"There's only one."

So Beverly asked Lewis what was on his mind, and when he told her she said, "Fine, that'd be fine, if you think there's a chance." There is no one so surprising as a good woman. They'd been married thirty years and still sometimes it embarrassed Lewis how much Beverly loved him.

That Texan, Oren Wright, was standing outside, hands jammed into his hip pockets. Lewis wondered if he'd looked so young back when he was courting Beverly.

"Penny. She gonna be all right?"

"She's sleeping now. It's a year ago today her daughter and husband were killed, you probably heard of it. They went off the road into a pond. Most years there's not much water in it, but we'd had a wet fall."

A handler paused then to say it was too bad about Penny's run, everybody admired how she'd brought Hope along and he'd been thinking of breeding his bitch to Hope.

"These things happen," Lewis said. "You seen Barlow?"

Ransome was by himself on the top row of the grandstand with his chin in his hand. Tommy Wilson was on the course with Roy.

Lewis sat beside him and after a minute he said, "Tommy's laying down a good run. I've always like that Roy dog."

As Roy went out for his second lot of sheep he crossed

over. A groan went up in the grandstand, and Florence Wilson, Tommy's wife, winced, visibly.

"He can't catch me now." Ransome stood, no longer interested.

"Sit down," Lewis said. "I got something to say to you."

Ransome said, "I don't like what happened any better'n you do. Was a time I thought that maybe me and Penny might have a chance together. Havin' her travel with me has brought dissatisfaction into my life and maybe I owe her for that. I don't like what happened to that dog either. Listen to him." A muffled howling, wild as a plains coyote. "I'm not sure I can put that dog back together again."

"I'll buy him back from you."

"It was a fair bet. I didn't force her into it. Things aren't so easy as that."

"I'll make you a wager," Lewis said. "Me and Nop haven't run. I don't expect we can catch you in the overall, but there's room to beat you today." Funny how cold Lewis felt, maybe the sun had gone behind a cloud. He clamped his jaw muscles to keep his teeth from chattering.

Ransome was pained. "Haven't you had enough? That dog of yours might have been a great dog once, but he's an old dog now. You won't beat me and then I'll have two Burkeholder dogs, one crazy as a loon, the other doddering around the trial field. Mr. Burkeholder, I don't mean to hurt your feelings, but I don't want your Nop dog, he's no use to me."

Lewis felt the heat climbing into his cheeks. "I don't generally wager for my dog," he said. "So long as Nop don't wager me, I don't wager him. You don't own a motor home."

Ransome Barlow eyed the Virginia farmer for a long time, blinking. "All you Burkeholders are nuts."

If Lewis won, he got Hope back. If Lewis lost; Lewis, Beverly, and Penny would go home in Ransome's old truck and Ransome'd take the keys to their motor home. "That dog is ruined," Ransome said. "He ain't ever gonna be any use again."

"Then it's a bet."

Ransome's handclasp was light and quick. Lewis would have expected more grip from the man.

IN THEIR MOTOR HOME, Beverly sat in the armchair, knitting woolen socks for the church clothing bank. Child's size, as always, and gaily striped in blues and reds and greens.

In back, Penny moaned. Ten minutes ago, Beverly had looked in on her, her hot brow, her wet hair matted against her forehead. Penny'd never get over it, Beverly knew. People don't ever get over it. They can only hope to find a new life in the center of their loss. Beverly decided to put a wavy blue line around the socks, exactly like the wavy blue line on her granddaughter Lisa's tennis shoes.

DOGS ARE NOTORIOUS for hope. Dogs believe that this morning, this very morning, may begin a day of fascination, easily grander than any day in the past. Perhaps the work did go badly yesterday, perhaps the humans are wild with sulks and rages, but *this* morning can yet be saved: don't humans understand anything?

Every morning, in dog pounds all over America, hundreds of dogs awake to their last day with gladness in their hearts.

. . .

WHEN OLD NOP WALKED onto that course, he knew what would be required of him, and hoped it would be within his powers. The sun had fallen behind the Bighorn Mountains, leaving a russet afterglow.

"Okay, partner," Lewis said, quietly, *"whhst."*

And Nop swung out, out, at nearly a ninety-degree angle from Lewis's feet, enjoying his body, the grass rushing beneath his feet, the air streaming along his face into his lungs, the sheer pleasure of exertion.

He slowed while the horsemen galloped away and then he slipped in behind the sheep: just so. Lewis's whistle said: "That's right, Nop." It said, "Thank you."

Ten sheep: Quickstep and Leader, Smelly Butt, Lulu, and six younger ewes who were followers. Nop told them to get along, and they did.

Lewis asked Nop to straighten Quickstep, who was drifting too far right, and Nop stepped over and said, "I don't think you understand who's in charge here."

And Quickstep hurried back into line saying, "Yes, sir, yes sir, three bags full." Nop was used to sheep saying foolish things.

They didn't want to go between the fetch gates, though the opening was plain, but sheep are spooky creatures and, well, it just didn't seem RIGHT doing it, so Nop trotted up behind them and pushed them through.

Now everything should be automatic: fetch the sheep to Lewis. But Lewis said, no, not this time. Go back. THINK ABOUT IT.

Lewis told Nop there were more woolies out here somewhere, though Nop couldn't see them. Nop did see horsemen, and since horsemen had meant sheep before, perhaps sheep were hiding with these horsemen too. When the horsemen trotted away Nop found five new woolies; Hardhead, and four younguns. They were skittish, but Nop warned Hardhead she'd do as he said or face consequences, dire but unspecified. Lewis asked Nop to bring both flocks together, and from then on, things proceeded normally, except Old Nop's legs were getting heavy by the time he brought the fifteen sheep into the hundred-foot shedding ring.

Young dogs flash through tiny openings between sheep like a knife cutting a cake and the sheep divide.

But old Nop didn't have the speed for that and his tongue was hanging out and his legs were shakey, so he stationed himself, motionless, on the far side of the shedding ring, and Lewis and he did a balancing act, pressuring the sheep, squeezing the flock until the desired sheep bolted away. "This one, Nop. No, *this* one, leave that one." And finally Lewis said, "That'll do, Nop," and though his legs were wobbling, Nop came in—not as fast as a young dog—and marched the proper sheep to the pen.

Time was Nop would have bullied those sheep into the pen. Now he stayed well back, adjusted himself to the proper angle and took a step forward, another. If Nop showed how weak he felt, Quickstep would have led her sheep to freedom. In the grandstand, people were checking their watches and whispering.

Quickstep saw her chance and bolted.

Like a young dog with fresh legs Old Nop blocked her. And the ewe tossed her nose in the air (I quit) and trotted into the pen and the others followed, and Lewis swung the gate closed, quick as he could, not much caring if he smacked a rump or not.

On the platform, the judge turned to the scorekeeper. "And how much time did he have left?"

"Two seconds."

"Well then," the judge said.

Lewis was kneeling beside Nop and touching his head. Lewis slung him in his arms and carried him off the course and laid him in the tub of cool water. It was minutes before Nop was able to lap at the water, and he paid no attention at all to the people standing around the stock tank or the flashing of their flashbulbs. He'd done his work.

NATIONAL HANDLERS' FINALS, CHAMPIONSHIP RUN

September 27, Sheridan, Wyoming
Judge: Stuart Davidson, Dunoon, Scotland

15 Open dogs went to the post. 120 points possible.

			Cumulative	Final ranking
1. Lewis Burkeholder	Nop	114	286	3
2. Ransome Barlow	Bute	112	296	1
3. Bill Berhow	Nick	108	287	2
4. Tom Wilson	Roy	108	276	4
5. Bruce Fogt	Molly	102	270	5
6. Dodie Green	Soot	98	266	6
7. Barbara Ligon	Mirk	98	265	7
8. Charles O'Reilly	Shep	94	259	9
9. Candy Kennedy	Sage	93	255	10
10. Pat Shannahan	Hannah	91	260	8
11. Dorrance Eikamp	Blue	90	250	12
12. Ralph Pulfer	Ken	90	251	11
13. Herbert Holmes	Dave	89	244	14
14. Red Oliver	Roy	88	248	13
15. Penny Burkeholder	Hope	DQ (0)	187	15

BY THE TIME the last dog ran, Penny had recovered enough to collect her fifteenth prize ribbon and prize money: $108.00. The *Working Border Collie News,* the *Ranch Dog Trainer,* even the *Billings Gazette* were taking the winners' pictures.

Lewis congratulated Ransome Barlow on winning the national championship.

"You're a lucky man, have a dog like Nop," Ransome said. "I never seen anything like that shed." He handed Lewis his prize check, already endorsed. "I'd appreciate it if you give this to your daughter. Tell her I'll send the rest of what I owe soon as I have it."

"I don't know what sort of arrangement you two made," Lewis said, "but I can't imagine she'd want you to starve yourself."

"I teach a clinic up in Great Falls next weekend, I'll be alright." Ransome looked Lewis straight in the eye. "I wish this had turned out otherwise for Penny and me. I never wanted no motor home. What do you get, eight miles a gallon? Hell, man like me can't afford a gas guzzler like that."

"Will you all face this way?" a photographer called. Obediently they reshuffled and Ransome Barlow and Bute moved to the left end of the photograph, which was how he appeared next morning in the *Billings Gazette,* holding his big wooden trophy. Bute looked out at the course like maybe if he stared long enough, he'd see some sheep.

OREN WRIGHT DROVE Penny's pickup back to Virginia. Lewis offered to spell him, but Oren refused. Penny rode in the motor home passenger seat all the way back, with Nop under her feet. Penny talked about Lisa and Mark and from time to time she'd cry.

Every morning, Beverly'd make up sandwiches. They didn't stop for lunch, just drove straight through. Hope traveled in a crate in Penny's pickup and was never outside except on a leash. Hope wouldn't raise his head or look anyone in the eye. Penny couldn't bear to be around him.

And so the Burkeholders drove back across the country on busy interstates, just another lumbering vehicle full of hopes and griefs and dreams. They came into their farm at dusk, and though their hired man had already fed, Lewis checked the stock before it got too dark, and Penny and Oren Wright and Beverly had coffee in the kitchen.

"You'll stay a day or two, Mr. Wright? We surely do thank you for driving across the country." That was Beverly.

"I'd hate to put you out." That was Oren.

"Don't be a dope." Penny, of course.

So Oren remained a week, helping Lewis with the farm work, taking meals with the family. Sunday, he accompanied the family to church and after services was introduced to Preacher Shumway, who said he'd never been to Texas.

"It's warmer," Oren said.

Oren never spent a moment alone with Penny, and when he asked her would she come down and lamb out for him again, he asked in front of her parents, the morning Lewis was to drive him to the airport.

"I haven't got a dog," Penny said.

"You've got Hope," Oren said.

"We're quits. He can't forgive me. I'm not sure he should."

Two days after Christmas, Penny left for Texas. She planned to spend an extra day in Alabama where Ted Johnson had a nice young dog for sale.

In February, every year, the missions committee of Beverly's church accompanied Preacher Shumway to Cap Balout, a village in the mountains of Haiti. There the Americans helped Father Père Galliard repair his modest dispensary and improve the village water supply. Several in the missions committee were learning Haitian patois, and one woman told Beverly, "You don't know all we've got until you see what it's like down there."

Beverly had never been out of the continental United States. After he dropped her at Dulles Airport, Lewis stopped at Wendy's for a bacon cheeseburger. Beverly had left him twenty-three home-cooked meals in the freezer, one for each day she'd be gone and two extra in case somebody stopped over.

"Beverly," he'd asked, "who in the world would stop over?"

Lewis didn't feel like a home-cooked meal, he felt like a bacon cheeseburger.

When Lewis got home, he went to the barn where Hope had stayed except for walks twice every day, on lead, since he came back from Wyoming. Hope'd had time to think.

"Well, son," Lewis said, "you 'bout done foolin' around?"

Hope stopped wagging his tail.

"We got ourselves just three weeks before Beverly comes home. It's slack time for farm work. How about I take you out tonight and work you on the young ewes, and from now on, you sleep in the house like Nop. That agreeable?"

Hope's eyes were unafraid.

"I'm going to be needing a second stockdog. Nop's the boss dog, but he needs help from time to time, and I'd like a young dog to run in the trials. I'm not out to be a national champion, just run some of the weekend trials, leave home in the morning, back before dark, what do you say?"

"I am thy stockdog," Hope said.

SPRING FLING SHEEPDOG TRIAL

March 13, Williamsville, Virginia
Judge: Tom Forrester, Aldie, Virginia

16 Open dogs went to the post

1.	Lewis Burkeholder	Nop	91
2.	Lewis Burkeholder	Hope	91 (Decided on outwork)
3.	Carla King	Pride	90
4.	Judy Mason	Nell	89
5.	Wink Mason	Buff	88

A Note to the Reader

Border Collies are bred to do exacting work at great distances from their handler. They are intelligent, obsessive, and physically powerful. Their handler needs both savvy and grit. Border Collies are not bred to be pets and those decent, caring, well-meaning people who buy a Border Collie pup for a pet are courting sorrow.

About the Author

Donald McCaig has been awarded a fellowship by the National Endowment for the Arts, the Prix Literaire by the Societe Protectrice des Animaux, and multiple awards by the Dog Writers Association of America. He recalls that fall afternoon in 1987 when he and his dog, Pip, came in fifth at the Edgeworth Open Sheep Dog Trial. They beat some pretty good dogs that day.